W.i.t.c.h.

Will Irma Taranee Cornelia Hay Lin

Out of the Dark

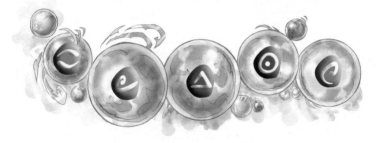

Adapted by JULIE KOMORN

HYPERION/ DISNEY
New York

© 2004 Disney Enterprises, Inc.

W.I.T.C.H. Will Irma Taranee Cornelia Hay Lin is a trademark of Disney Enterprises, Inc.
The Volo colophon is a trademark of Disney Enterprises, Inc.
Volo® is a registered trademark of Disney Enterprises, Inc.

Printed in the United States of America
First Edition
1 3 5 7 9 10 8 6 4 2

This book is set in 12/16.5 Hiroshige Book.
ISBN 0-7868-1797-6
Visit www.clubwitch.com

AFTER ALL, WE'RE WORKING WITH WATERCOLORS. AND SINCE YOU DO CONTROL THE POWER OF WATER . . . IT SHOULDN'T BE TOO DIFFICULT FOR YOU!

GOOD POINT, TARANEE!

I THINK THAT IS CALLED CHEATING!

OH, LIGHTEN UP! THERE'S NOTHING WRONG WITH WANTING A GOOD GRADE IN DRAWING. JUST THINK HOW IMPRESSED MRS. WHARTON WILL BE!

HERE WE GO. . . . IT'S WORKING. . . . IT'S REALLY WORKING!

DRIIIIIN

SCHOOL IS OVER FOR THE DAY.

SO WHAT ARE YOU UP TO THIS AFTERNOON?

BESIDES STUDYING? NOT MUCH! I MIGHT GO WITH MY MOM TO LOOK FOR A NEW PAIR OF SKATES! I'M A LITTLE BEHIND WITH MY TRAINING, AND IT WOULD BE A GOOD EXCUSE TO START AGAIN.

WHAT ABOUT YOU?

STUDYING, STUDYING, AND MORE STUDYING.

ONE

Will Vandom shifted the position of her pink backpack. It was loaded up with textbooks—and it was *heavy*. Walking home from school with her four best friends, Cornelia, Irma, Hay Lin, and Taranee, Will wondered what she would do without them.

Those friends were basically the first people she had met when she moved to Heatherfield at the beginning of the school year, and they'd made her feel right at home. Now the five of them were like fingers on a hand—all very different from one another, yet connected in a very important way.

Their differences were quite apparent—Cornelia's long, blond hair and self-confidence, Irma's smirk and sassiness, Hay

Lin's long, silky pigtails and sweet, easygoing smile, and Taranee's wild braids and mellow hipness. What connected the girls, however, was more than skin-deep: They all had magic powers.

Sometimes Will still couldn't believe it.

As they passed over piles of snow covering the sidewalks, Will gazed over at Taranee, whose sparkling brown eyes, with long, dark lashes, peeked out from her round specs. She wore an orange dress with funky stripes, a cool, beige jacket, ankle socks, and clogs. Taranee was sweet and down-to-earth and sometimes a bit shy. Will guessed that that was why Taranee was so crazy about photography—she could capture the action around her without having to be the center of attention.

As the girls turned a corner, Will looked over at Hay Lin and smiled. Hay Lin was always ready with a big grin. She was carefree and full of enthusiasm about the world around her. A talented artist and a funky dresser, she even had her very own look. Today's special featured a fuzzy, pink zip-up sweater, extra-baggy jeans, a sporty messenger bag, two-toned sneakers, a gray jacket, and matching bubble goggles on her head. A definite fashion diva–in–training, thought Will, with a laugh.

And then there was Irma—the jokester in the group. Will could see Irma being a stand-up comedian one day. Or maybe a hotshot Hollywood record producer, since Irma loved listening to music. Today, her wavy, auburn hair was pulled into pigtails and chock-full of kitty-shaped barrettes. Her big, blue, mischievous eyes sparkled as she stood there in her blue sweater, wide-cuffed brown pants, and comfy-looking, zippered jacket. Irma was a definite goofball, mused Will, but her sense of fun was irresistible.

While the rest of them were stumbling over mounds of snow, Will noticed that Cornelia gracefully floated over the snow, without breaking her stride. You could practically tell she was a champion figure skater by the way she carried herself. Cornelia was also really smart— she questioned everything, in a logical, no-nonsense, thoughtful way. Today she sported a pink turtleneck, purple, knitted cap, and as always, a long, flowing skirt. Across her brown, faux fur–trimmed coat, she carried a maroon shoulder bag, and dangling from the strap was a little, plastic, roly-poly, googly-eyed, toy key chain. Cornelia wasn't *always* serious.

Yeah, Will's friends were great—really awesome, in fact. The only problem was that, at this particular moment, each one of them was in a cranky mood. So, if the five of them were like the fingers on a hand, Will mused, then today, that hand was more like a fist.

And even though everyone had pretty much made up by the time they had left the school yard, a bit of tension still hung in the air. Plus, Will could tell that something else, besides Irma, was bugging Cornelia.

Will admitted to herself that she wasn't in the best of moods, either. She had homework up to her eyeballs and couldn't help being overwhelmed at the thought of it.

A cool breeze whizzed by. Will felt cozy in her puffy, navy-blue coat, thick socks, and fur-lined boots.

And there was actually some good news, too, Will thought, excitement building in her. No, make that amazing, fantastic, incredible news. Will and her friends were going to the Karmilla concert on Sunday!

Will couldn't wait. And the best part of it

all? Matt's band, Cobalt Blue, was going to be the opening act for the night's concert.

Ah, Matt. Will blushed just thinking about him. She had a major crush on that boy. Matt was one year older than Will and, without question, the biggest hunk in school. He was totally dreamy. With his brown hair, tall, lanky body, superstrong jawline, and scruffy goatee, he fit the role of lead singer and major hottie perfectly.

School, homework, friends, crushes—all of it made for another normal day in Heatherfield. But the truth was that nothing was really very normal in Heatherfield. . . .

Will remembered when it had all started— the time she had first noticed her magic powers. She had been riding her bike down the street and seen her reflection in a bookstore window. She had been stunned by what she saw. It was her reflection, but in a transformed, enhanced, mature version—*and* she had sprouted wings.

It turned out that all five friends had been given magical powers. Cornelia had control over the earth. Hay Lin was all about air. Taranee was friends with fire. And Irma manipulated all things related to water.

And Will held the key to all those powers—which made her the leader of the group. (Will didn't like to talk about it; she still wasn't sure about her leadership role.) As leader, she was the Keeper of the Heart of Candracar, a glowy, crystal orb that popped out of her palm when she needed it. And every time Will unleashed the pink, glowing orb, she and her friends all turned into winged, fierce, don't-mess-with-us girls.

They even had a group name for themselves—W.i.t.c.h., an acronym made up of their first names: Will, Irma, Taranee, Cornelia, and Hay Lin.

Will and her friends soon discovered that there was a whole bunch of other worlds floating around out there beyond earth. One of those worlds was Metamoor, a dark, Gothic place inhabited by talking, blue-and-green monsters. It was a land that had been taken over by evil. And that was why the all-knowing Oracle of Candracar had created the Veil, which was a sort of barrier that separated Metamoor from earth.

Will stopped to tie her shoelace and looked up at Cornelia's big, heart-shaped face. Cornelia's pink-glossed lips were set in a tight, tense line. She really missed Elyon and wanted her friends to give Elyon another chance.

Elyon Brown had been a friend of the girls'. But as soon as they had been handed their mission as Guardians of the Veil, Elyon had traveled through a portal, never to return.

Elyon had tried all sorts of dirty tricks to harass Will and her friends. She'd teased and tormented them and then almost really hurt them, with the help of some weird, wiggling brick walls. Finally, she'd kidnapped Taranee and deceived her into believing that her friends had forgotten her. Soon afterward, the Guardians had rushed to Metamoor and rescued Taranee.

After all of that, how could Will trust Elyon? Will didn't know Elyon as well as Cornelia did, and she just wasn't able to forgive and forget as easily.

"Remember what she did to Taranee, and all those traps she set for us?" Will cried after seeing Cornelia's expression. "She is the enemy, Cornelia. You can't forget that!"

"But she was my best friend," Cornelia explained. "And when I was in Meridian, she helped me. You don't know her like I do."

Irma interrupted. "Well, I have to go this way," she said casually, raising an eyebrow and turning away. It was obvious that she wanted an easy escape from the tense conversation.

"I'll come with you," Taranee said quickly, throwing her multicolored, kente-cloth bag over her shoulder. She was another one who'd had enough controversy for one day.

With a brief wave and a sympathetic smile, Hay Lin joined Irma and Taranee for the walk home. Her long black pigtails danced behind her back as she turned to go.

Cornelia was clearly bummed at her three friends' leaving. "We are never going to solve the problem this way," she called after them. "We need to talk about it."

But apparently, this wasn't the right time.

Cornelia shrugged her shoulders and continued walking with Will.

"Do you feel the same way, Will?" Cornelia asked.

Will was definitely confused. "It's hard to say, Cornelia," she answered. "But from what I've seen . . ."

"I'm positive that Elyon got caught up in

something beyond her control," Cornelia said firmly. "Maybe she needs our help."

The two of them strolled toward Will's apartment building.

"Why can't we give her the benefit of the doubt and forgive her?" she continued. "You just forgave Irma."

"It's not the same thing, and you know it," Will answered.

"Can't you promise to just think about it?" Cornelia suggested, as they now stood in front of Will's building.

"I promise," said Will, squeezing Cornelia's hands and looking into her eyes. "See you later, Cornelia."

Just at that moment, Will's mom pulled up in her red car and parked in front of the building. "Will!" her mom cried cheerfully. Will was happy—and surprised—to see her. Her mom rarely got home from the office that early. She worked crazy hours as a consultant at a huge, swanky, computer technology company called Simultech.

"Hi, Mom!" Will cried, after waving good-bye to Cornelia.

Her mom had popped open the trunk,

which was filled with grocery bags, and was starting to unload it. Will walked over to her mother and gave her a kiss hello.

"I'm glad you're here," her mom replied, struggling with the bags of groceries. "Could you give me a hand with these shopping bags? They weigh a ton."

"Ugh," Will said, picking up several bulky plastic bags and hauling them toward the front door of their apartment building. They were very heavy. Her mom followed behind carrying her own load, which included a large six-pack of bottled water.

"What's with all these groceries?" Will asked, peeking inside a bag containing fresh fruit, vegetables, homemade pasta, fancy cheese, and gourmet ice cream. Usually her mom just picked up a few things here or there for the two of them.

"It's for Sunday," her mom said with a big smile as they approached their apartment. "I want the party to be perfect." Her mom slid the key in and opened the door.

"The . . . party?" Will asked once they were inside. Her voice echoed throughout their loft-style apartment. Is there something I'm forgetting? she wondered, suddenly panicking. Will followed her mom straight into the kitchen and placed the bags on the breakfast table.

"Don't tell me you forgot?" Her mom looked stunned. "It's my birthday!"

"Of course I didn't forget," Will said, although it had in fact slipped her mind for a minute. She felt a bit embarrassed. "It's . . . it's just that I didn't think you were having a party."

"It's a private lunch party, actually," her mom explained with a grin. "Just for the two of us. Isn't that great?" She pulled a carton of milk and a jar of pickles from the bag in front of her. "And then afterward, we'll take a trip to Roseville," she continued. "It's been so long since we did anything fun like that." She sounded excited.

Roseville was a charming little town with antiques shops, art galleries, cozy cafés, and funky clothing stores. Back when Will and her mom had lived in Fadden Hills, they had used to hang out in Roseville whenever they had the chance.

Her mother placed the cheese, soda, and vegetables inside the fridge. Will pulled a chair over so she could stand on it and reach the cupboard. Birthdays were a funny thing, she thought, as she put away the cereal, crackers, and cookies. There were some people who really didn't care about them (or at least pretended not to). And then there were people who liked to make a big deal out of them. Her mom was definitely a big-deal birthday person.

Wow. This wasn't going to be easy, Will thought.

Will turned to her mother apprehensively. "It's a fantastic idea, Mom," she said enthusiastically. "There's just one little problem." She closed the cupboard and climbed down from the chair. They were now eye to eye. "I can't do it this Sunday. There's a concert in town and my friends and I are going. Irma's dad is bringing us—"

"I had really hoped to spend the day with you," her mom interrupted. Her face looked serious, and a little hurt.

"We can always go to Roseville next weekend," Will offered, trying to sound hopeful.

"Next weekend it won't be my birthday anymore," her mom scowled, crossing her arms. "I'm sorry, Will."

Boy, she sure is being firm, Will thought, rubbing her head.

"We never see each other anymore," her mom continued. "You spend all your time alone or with your friends."

"What am I supposed to do?" Will cried out with frustration. "It's not my fault you're never here."

"I have to work, Will!" her mom answered angrily. "You always seem to forget that."

"I know!" Will yelled back. "But you always manage to find time for Mr. Collins, don't you?" The last part came out harshly, and Will knew she shouldn't have said it, but it had just slipped out. Part of her didn't care that she was acting like a brat, however. She was upset, and the whole conversation seemed majorly unfair.

Mr. Collins was a teacher at Will's school that her mom had been dating. Yes, dating. And it was definitely a touchy subject between them. The idea of her mom dating was weird enough, but her mom dating her history teacher?

Sure, he was a nice enough guy, but that was beside the point. The whole thing made Will feel really uncomfortable.

The last comment about Mr. Collins had

really set her mom off. She stood with her hands on her hips, staring at Will.

"Don't use that tone with me!" she ordered, looking both worried and angry. "With the way things are between us, Sunday's schedule will now be a little different." She took a deep breath and glared at Will, her big brown eyes practically popping out of her head.

Will's face turned red as nervousness spread throughout her body.

"You will *not* go to the concert," her mom continued, now enraged. "And I *won't* give any party! We'll stay here at home in silence." As a parting shot, her mom added, "The conversation is over!"

They both fell silent. Will stood like a statue—she couldn't believe what she was hearing. Could her mom actually be that mean? Will stared back at her, tears welling up in her eyes. She was pouting big-time.

Will turned away from her mother, stormed up the stairs, and stomped down the hall into her bedroom, slamming the door behind her. Leaning back, with her shoulders up against the tall, wooden door, she sobbed.

Through her tears she noticed piles of books

and heaps of clothes strewn across her room. And everywhere she looked were members of her enormous toy-frog collection—you could practically hear a chorus of "ribbets." But at that particular moment none of those adorable green frog dolls or knickknacks could snap her out of her funk.

She stopped crying just long enough to notice something moving around on the floor. It was her pet dormouse—the one Matt had encouraged her to bring home. The small, brown, fuzzy animal was happily chewing on one of her plush frog puppets. It looked up at her with the frog between its teeth. The puppet was almost as big as the dormouse was.

Will plopped facedown on her bed, burying her face in the pillow. She felt all out of sorts; she couldn't believe that she would be missing the Karmilla concert. It was so unfair! She felt confused about what had just happened with her mother. And there was that whole thing with Cornelia and Elyon, too. There were way too many issues to deal with. What was the right thing to do? She couldn't help thinking about how much her life had changed over the last few months. She felt totally alone.

Will noticed that her dormouse had crawled over and jumped on her bed. It looked up curiously at her for a moment, with a sweet expression on its face. Will raised her head to look at it. Her head felt heavy from all of the crying. The dormouse crept over to Will and stuck its little nose in her face. *"Eeeek?"* it squealed softly.

She huddled over on her side, took her pet in her arms, and hugged it closely to her chest. The dormouse curled up between her arms affectionately. A smile worked its way across her face, but her eyes were still full of tears.

TWO

The Temple of Candracar stood still and peaceful in the midst of its grandeur. A delicate light shimmered across the ornate, white spires and endless arches, past heavenly towers and soaring walkways.

The Temple was the very center of all magical worlds—a mystical palace in the middle of infinity. Powerful spirits and creatures lived there, and their job was to protect the harmony of the universe. Encircling this special place was a silvery substance both lighter than air and purer than water.

The Oracle was the leader of the Congregation of Candracar. He was the benevolent, all-knowing being who had anointed the five girls as Guardians of the Veil. And while he looked boyish, the Oracle was actually old and wise, and he always knew what was happening.

He now stood tranquilly in an enormous room with a vaulted ceiling. Tibor, the Oracle's faithful adviser, was positioned behind him, always ready to obey. He was full of undying trust in the Oracle, understanding his wisdom and ready to defend him at all costs.

An immense, misty cloud of pure air cascaded and curled toward them.

The Oracle gazed out peacefully through the big, arched window at the cosmic view of the grounds that surrounded the Temple. Tibor looked, too. They looked inside the town of Heatherfield to check on the Guardians. The Oracle turned his attention to Will, who he saw was home, huddled in her bed, crying.

The Oracle remained calm, even though the scene below revealed the girl's unhappiness and frustration.

"Will feels alone. . . ." the Oracle softly commented to Tibor. "I would like to help her, but I cannot." His infinite wisdom allowed him always to believe in the good of the universe— to understand and accept others' uncertainties and feelings. But for a moment, a hint of sadness flickered across his usually stoic face.

"I probably shouldn't say this, Tibor," he said. "But sometimes I feel a little guilty. Will and her friends are so young for such a large responsibility."

Tibor rubbed his long, white beard. "They are the Guardians of the Veil, Oracle," he replied, looking out kindly from under his bushy eyebrows. "The story has always been the same. After a rough start, they have always completed their tasks."

The Oracle left off gazing at Will and glided further inside the Temple to the sacred space. Tibor followed him.

The Oracle assumed the lotus pose, hovering effortlessly on a current of air. His thoughts focused on Tibor's remark about the Guardians' tasks. Lilies floated beneath him in a pool of serene water. "This is true. . . ." he said thoughtfully, his robe flowing out beneath him. "But at what price?"

THREE

It's good to be a prince, thought Phobos.

I'm the powerful leader of Meridian, he mused proudly. He had to admit that he had it pretty good.

He stood tall inside his colossal palace. His long, blue-and-white, royal robes hung down from his wide shoulders and floated out around him. His crown, a ridged triangle set with turquoise stones, extended right down between his brows, accenting his intense, slate-blue eyes.

Phobos looked down at the city.

Meridian was in worse shape than ever, he noticed. A dark sky dominated the dusky, Gothic metropolis. Gloomy streams of fog hung over the frail, doomed buildings, the crumbling, covered passageways, and the jagged, cobblestoned streets. Rows of decrepit, stone homes with droopy rooftops could be seen in every direction. It was a scene of medieval urban sprawl.

But none of that was of concern to Phobos.

His palace sat high upon a hill, away from the center of the city. It was a lush dreamland, surrounded by magical vegetation and a protective barrier of black roses. Inside his fortress a strong, fierce light shone across vaulted ceilings, gilded columns, and abundantly jeweled walls.

Quite a difference from the crumbling, dilapidated buildings below, he smirked to himself.

The palace was so nice, in fact, that Phobos never left it. He locked himself inside and showed himself only through his faithful Murmurers. The Murmurers were creatures that Phobos had turned from real flowers into flowerlike wraiths. They were his eyes, ears, and voice—they were his only connection to his people. They ensured that lowly commoners kept their distance from him. Phobos preferred it like that.

The Murmurers sat perched inside petals. Their long hair, made of vines and branches, sprouted in every direction, covering their striped bodies. Their fierce, pink-and-blue faces poked out with wide, unblinking stares, reflecting the same intense evil as that of their leader.

Yes, Phobos was quite content here in his castle. He rubbed his red goatee, remembering his victory—it had been quite a while now since he had usurped the throne of Meridian. He was proud to be the first man to rule—before him, only queens had reigned. But they had all disappeared, and now Phobos, the true leader of Meridian, was in charge.

Right now, his power was the strongest it had ever been. A smile spread across his sharp, chiseled face. It was because he had absorbed all of the powers of Meridian. All of that power allowed him to create his very own, personal paradise. He paced up and down the length of the room, admiring its splendor. So what if the rest of Meridian had been reduced to the most wretched level of misery? he thought with a laugh. He was living like a king—and that was all that mattered.

But now he had a new goal.

Phobos wanted to rule over other worlds, too, so that he could acquire even more power. Phobos had already absorbed all the energy and magic in Metamoor in order to live. Now he needed other worlds to absorb. His target now was earth—not Candracar, not the Oracle, not his Congregation. And that plan made Phobos all the more dangerous.

There were only two—well six—things in his way. The Veil and the five Guardians.

And Phobos intended to eliminate all of them. Ever since the new millennium, the Veil had been weakened, which had made things quite easy for the evil prince. He just needed to get large numbers of creatures from Meridian to cross through the Veil at one time. All of those creatures leaving at one time would immediately weaken the Veil even more—and pretty much destroy it.

But those Guardians . . . they were a different story.

Phobos was growing impatient with the five earth girls—all that goodness, that youthful spirit, all those colorful outfits and wings—ugh, it made him sick just thinking about it! And what did they know, anyway? Up to that point they had just been lucky. But Phobos knew that their luck would soon run out.

Some, he mused, might have called his plan ruthless. Even evil, perhaps. But to Phobos it was just a matter of taking the necessary steps to get what he deserved. Could he help it if he had an unquenchable thirst for power?

Phobos turned from the window. His long, thick, blond braids extended out in all directions from his head down his back.

Speaking of power, Phobos was grateful to have Lord Cedric to help him attain his goals. Cedric was the commander of the elite warriors in Phobos's Royal Guard.

Phobos had summoned Cedric to the palace—and Cedric was knocking at that very moment. Phobos ordered the doors to be opened, allowing Cedric access to his private chamber.

Cedric entered and bowed to Phobos, dropping to his knees. His long, blond hair fell loosely over his shoulders. Today he appeared in his human form, rather than the green, reptilian persona that he had been sporting lately. He tilted his head forward toward Phobos, showing his respect. His eyes glinted like sapphires, and his skin was porcelain-smooth. He looked too handsome to be as bad as he was.

Cedric was there to talk about the recent battle in Meridian—and how the rebels had defeated Phobos's army.

Phobos noticed that Cedric was nervous standing before him. As Cedric continued talking, Phobos realized that he was trying to hide his humiliation. Nobody liked to lose a battle.

While it made Phobos angry that they had lost, he would never show his disappointment to Cedric. Anyway, as far as Phobos was concerned, the fighting wasn't over just yet.

Cedric was attempting to explain why he and the soldiers had lost to the Meridian rebels. But both he and Phobos knew it was due to the efforts of the Guardians—those five girls who had helped crush his army. Those girls were always thwarting his plans. Every time one of Phobos's creatures tried to cross a portal, the girls showed up to foil the plan. He was getting pretty tired of them.

Cedric continued to blather on about the battle. Phobos already knew it all—he was the ruler, after all—but he listened to Cedric's excuses. He loved to watch him squirm.

But enough was enough. "What you say worries me, my loyal Cedric," Phobos interrupted. He paused dramatically. "All of our efforts to get the Guardians of the Veil in trouble have backfired! My patience is wearing thin." He glared at Cedric. So did the Murmurers.

Prince Phobos walked down from his throne and stood in front of Cedric, towering over him. Phobos had red jewels decorating his forehead, and he liked the way their radiance practically blinded Cedric.

"And I wouldn't want to think I made a mistake putting you in charge of this task," Phobos continued menacingly. He rubbed his hands together a bit compulsively and strolled around the room. The Murmurers surrounded him. Their voices were like a hypnotic chant.

"You have made no mistakes, Your Highness. . . ." Cedric burst out. His voice sounded confident, but his eyes were filled with fear.

"I know," the prince said icily, in a near whisper. The Murmurers moved aside, restless but full of respect for the prince. "But time is running out." Phobos gazed down at Cedric with a cold stare. "And worse still, my sister is becoming suspicious!"

Elyon was Phobos's long-lost sister. He had put Cedric in charge of luring her from earth to Meridian and keeping her there. So far, so good.

For Phobos to reach his ultimate goal, he needed Elyon. He needed to absorb her powers—she was the lawful heir to the throne of Metamoor and had immense power within her. Phobos had a plan—it was to take place at the upcoming coronation ceremony. And poor Elyon had no idea she wasn't going to be a princess. Phobos couldn't help letting out a sinister chuckle at the thought of it.

Phobos walked over to the window and parted the heavy curtains covering the wide terrace. A bright light flooded in from outside.

"It's time to leave Meridian," Phobos said purposefully. The murmuring vines with their wild leaves curled up behind him.

Phobos stepped onto the terrace, gesturing down toward the city. Cedric stood behind him, peeking over his shoulder. The city looked as chaotic and troubled as ever.

"Look at it, Cedric!" Phobos exclaimed.

"Meridian is turning off—slowing down! I've absorbed all its energy and natural resources."

Phobos's gaze landed on the main street of the town. He scowled at the ruined buildings and dirty streets. He spotted some thorny, green Meridian monsters bent over and limping, wearing rags.

"And now the people are beginning to fade, because of poverty and other difficulties," he snickered.

He looked inside the house of a Meridian family. He saw the misery of their lives as a sad, blue-faced mother, father, and child sat around a table eating bowls of cold porridge. Water dripped from their ceiling onto their table and down to a puddle on the floor.

"Stopping the people's frustration is no longer possible," Phobos explained. "And that is why my plan is so perfect!" He turned around to face Cedric.

"You'll encourage the people of Meridian to get even more angry, more frustrated!" he ordered, crossing his arms. "I want their hate and desperation to grow."

"But, Your Highness," Cedric said, hesitating. "Why?"

"When they hate me enough, they will do anything to escape from my rule," Phobos cackled. "Then, you will send them through the Veil, forcing them through a new portal."

"I don't understand," Cedric responded quietly. He looked worried and frightened.

Phobos noticed Cedric gazing up at the Murmurers with worry. Their faces were severe and judging, just like Phobos's.

"The Veil is the only thing that stands in the way of freedom," the Murmurers buzzed, pronouncing the words of Phobos along with him. "*My* freedom," he emphasized. "A massive attack will cause it to fall apart—break down. Its structure is weak with age."

Phobos gave an evil, satisfied laugh. "And the force of all the people will destroy it," he continued, his voice booming gravely. "Fighting against the Guardians of Candracar is useless!"

Cedric, who now stood at a distance, carefully listened to every word Phobos said. He was petrified.

Phobos shot Cedric a sidelong glance. "The consequences will be catastrophic for earth. But no conquest is complete without pain!"

Phobos turned and walked closer toward

Cedric, staring him feverishly in the eye. He wanted Cedric to understand the urgency of the situation.

"So, my dear Cedric," Phobos commanded, his cold, marblelike eyes peering down at his servant. "Do not fail me this time!"

And with that, Phobos turned and began to fade into the blinding light, the Murmurers disappearing right along with him. But just before leaving, Phobos glanced back at Cedric.

There Cedric sat, alone in the empty room, atop the marshy ground of low-growing flowers and mushrooms. As Cedric tilted his head back and lifted his hand to his eyes to block out the harsh light, the curtains flittered around the window's edge.

The light enveloped Phobos completely. He couldn't help grinning. His perfect plan was almost in place.

FOUR

Ugh, thought Hay Lin. What a drag.

She hated having to choose between her friends and her family. They both meant the world to her. What to do, what to do? . . . She took a deep breath.

But if there were ever a perfect place to sit and think, it was in her bedroom. Hay Lin found it to be the most pleasant spot on earth. Sure it was a mess, but she liked to think of it as her creative zone—her very own art studio.

She looked around at all the paintbrushes and watercolors and colored pencils scattered about. It seemed as though every patch of wall were covered with either a drawing, a painting, or a collage. She even had a corkboard displaying sketches of her

latest fashion designs (all were signed *Hay Lin*, with a little heart over the *i*). And strewn across her floor were various teen catalogs, comic books, and fashion magazines.

It was definitely cozy in here, thought Hay Lin.

She let out a sigh. She knew the right thing to do—but it sure wasn't fun.

She picked up her orange phone from its cradle and plopped onto her bed.

Within a few seconds, she had her friend on the line.

She heard a drawn-out gasp on the other end when she started to explain.

"Believe me, Irma," Hay Lin said, flopping back onto her pillow. "I'm sorrier than you!"

Irma was silent.

"It's just a mild case of the flu," Hay Lin explained, placing her palm on her forehead as if feeling for a fever. "But I'd rather be safe than sorry."

Sunday had finally arrived. Hay Lin and her friends had waited all week for this very day. And now Hay Lin had to cancel at the last minute. She was seriously bumming.

She played with a few of the bungee cords

she had wrapped around her waist. "I'll be there for the next concert, okay?" she added cheerfully.

"First Will, and now you!" Irma grumbled through the phone. "What's going on with you guys? This was going to be the greatest day ever. A chance like this doesn't happen every day."

Irma sure wasn't making this easy.

Hay Lin could hear Irma's father's gruff voice in the background. "Let's go, Irma, we're going to be late!"

Hay Lin cuddled her green alien doll in her arms and gave it a good, comforting squeeze.

"Your loss, Hay Lin," Irma said jokingly. "And even though you don't deserve it, I'll get you some autographs. Hope you feel better!" she added kindly.

Hay Lin said good-bye to Irma and hung up—*tlic*. She placed the phone on her desk next to a stack of papers, newspapers, and recent drawings.

I don't like lying to my friends, she thought. . . . but if I told them the truth they would have made fun of me *forever*.

Hay Lin got up out of bed and stretched for a minute before standing up. She wore a comfy, red, hooded pullover, green jeans, and pink, strappy clogs. She had cords wrapped around her wrists in a cool, crisscrossed pattern. To skip out on a concert just to help your parents was a pretty lame thing, she thought. Which was why she was covering up.

But until Mom starts feeling better, it's what I've got to do.

Her mom was actually the one with the flu. So, right now, her family had to come first.

Hay Lin left her bedroom and headed down the hall, her long, blue-black pigtails sailing behind her.

Times like these made her miss her grandmother.

Her grandmother had passed away several months before, but Hay Lin would never forget her.

Hay Lin remembered the time when Will, Irma, Taranee, and Cornelia had been over at her house munching on cookies and talking about their wacky dreams. All of them had had the same dream about the magical Heart of Candracar. Her grandmother had walked into the room and shown them the real Heart. She had told them they were Guardians of the Veil.

It had been pretty surreal. And it turned out that her grandmother had once been a Guardian of the Veil, too.

Hay Lin also would never forget the day when her grandmother had given her the map of the twelve portals. Her grandmother had been sick in bed and Hay Lin had stopped into her room to say hello. That was when Hay Lin's grandmother had handed her the rolled-up, raggedy-edged map. When Hay Lin had unrolled the parchment, the whole town of Heatherfield had come to life, showing where the passageways to Meridian were.

Her grandmother had always known what was going on. She had been a special, wise woman. And she had been strong. Hay Lin tried to summon that strength right now so she wouldn't feel so bad about being away from her friends.

Hay Lin poked her head into her parents' bedroom to check in on her mom.

There her mom sat, wrapped in a blanket, resting in a big, comfy, wicker armchair. Next to her were a box of tissues, a paperback, her favorite red teapot—the one with the tiny partridge perched on the lid—and a cup of steaming, hot tea. Even when she was under the weather, she still looked pretty, in her lavender-and-purple bathrobe, with a pink scarf tied around her neck. Her hair was pulled back in a bun with a flower barrette clipped in. A few loose strands hung down around her face.

"Ah-choo!" Her mom's sneeze was so strong Hay Lin was afraid she might break the china vases displayed on the corner shelf.

"Don't get too close, Hay Lin," she sniffled. "I think I'm a little infectious." Hay Lin looked out the window behind her mom. The sky was cloudy and gray.

Beneath the floorboards, Hay Lin could hear the faint din of her parents' restaurant—the Silver Dragon: broad-bladed cleavers chopping vegetables, food steaming in woks, and customers yucking it up—those were sounds she'd grown up with, and they were as comforting to her as a mug of hot chocolate or a big, fuzzy sweater.

"All right, Mom. I'll be downstairs," Hay Lin said, giving her mother a concerned look. "If you need anything, call me."

Hay Lin skipped down the stairs in her energetic way. She smiled at the noise her clogs made on the wooden steps. *Thump, thump*, and *thump*—She took a deep whiff, inhaling the delightful garlic and ginger scents coming from the kitchen.

The stairs led straight to the back entrance to the restaurant. Hay Lin stood behind the door marked *Private* and pulled back the red curtains. She peeked out at the dining room, adorned with vases, good-luck cat figurines, celadon walls, red paper lanterns, and fresh flowers. The restaurant was absolutely packed—every table was full, and a small crowd had gathered at the entrance waiting to be seated. And there was Hay Lin's father, wearing his chef's hat and apron, taking two customers' orders. He peered down over his reading glasses as he scribbled on a notepad, looking befuddled.

"I think I may be a little confused," he said, apologetically. "Did you order the fried ice cream?"

"Actually," said a man in a red argyle vest, "we have been waiting for the spring rolls for half an hour. . . ." With a forced smile the customer added, "But at this point, the fried ice cream will be fine. We're starving."

Her father, who was usually cool, calm, and collected, was visibly frazzled. Something tells me that the one who really needs me is my father, Hay Lin thought.

She stuck her head back into the hot kitchen—which was complete chaos. There was Fang, their chef. He was a big, roly-poly guy with a baby face. "Aaargh!" he huffed, his thin mustache and expressive eyebrows quivering. "Whose order of rice is this?" A white, fluffy chef's hat covered his big, bald head, and a thin, black ponytail trailed down his back. "And make sure you keep that soup warm!"

"Here," Hay Lin said. "Let me help with that, Fang."

Hay Lin spotted a few cooks in the back wearing white shirts and bandannas, and sautéing and stirring. Bamboo steamers full of dumplings and platters full of egg rolls, chicken chow mein, sweet-and-sour shrimp, and moo shu pork waited on the edge of the counter, ready to be served. Wonton and hot-and-sour soups were ladled into bowls outfitted with ceramic spoons. Nearby were plates of freshly baked almond cookies.

At that moment, Hay Lin's father came back into the kitchen holding two bowls of fried rice with chopsticks stuck into them. He looked frantic. "Hay Lin, where have you been?" he asked. Without waiting for an answer, he quickly started handing out instructions. "Ring up the bill for table five and then take the orders for tables eight, ten, and twelve. Hurry!"

"Whew!" Hay Lin said, wrapping her Silver Dragon apron around her. "I've only been back on the job for three seconds, and already I want to take a break!"

Hay Lin picked up two red bowls of hot soup, trying carefully not to spill them. I bet Irma, Cornelia, and Taranee are having more fun than I am! she thought.

FIVE

Taranee could barely contain herself. Here she was at the Karmilla concert with her friends. Her first concert ever. Hel-*lo*, dream come true, she thought. She felt so grown up!

Could things get any better? Sure, she usually grooved on classical music, but Karmilla rocked. They were one of the hottest groups. And Cobalt Blue, the opening band, wasn't too shabby, either.

She couldn't believe her mom had actually let her go. It took just a little begging and pleading. Okay, a lot of begging and pleading, Taranee remembered. Her mom was way overprotective.

Taranee's mom was a judge. Maybe that was why she was always so controlling, thought Taranee. All day long, she had to sit and listen to stories of the crimes of thugs and criminals. It was a wonder she even let Taranee out of the house.

Taranee thought back to her recent date with her crush, Nigel. Her mom hadn't been so easygoing about that, either. Nigel was this really great guy—she swooned just thinking about his shaggy, brown hair; shiny, brown eyes; and clean-boy smell. But her mom hadn't liked him, because he had once been in this guy Uriah's wannabe gang, the Outfielders.

But Nigel wasn't a troublemaker at all. Shy, sweet, and incredibly kind was more like it. One time, he had left her a box with her name on it. When Taranee opened it, a beautiful butterfly had flown out. How amazing was that? But when Nigel had come to her house to pick her up, her mom had watched them like a hawk. Her mom hadn't liked the whole idea of the two of them together.

But even though her mom might not have been happy about it, Taranee was allowed out of the house. And Nigel and she had had a rollicking snowball fight and then seen a really fun movie. It had been a perfect night indeed.

Now, here she was on another perfect, special night. Irma's father, who was in charge of security at the concert, led Taranee, Irma, and Cornelia through the stadium entrance. They passed lines of fans stretching around the stadium who looked as if they had been waiting for hours. The parking lot was packed with limos, cars, trucks, motorcycles, vans, and tour buses.

Taranee gaped at the crowd streaming into the lobby alongside them—Karmilla fans of all ages, colors, shapes, and sizes, many of the girls decked out in tight clothes, with full makeup.

And then Irma's father pulled out the backstage passes. Boy, did Taranee feel important as she and her friends approached the doors marked *No Entrance*. Without anyone saying a word, they glided past the extra-large security guards.

Once they were backstage, Taranee and her friends looked around with astonishment. They watched the slew of odd characters around them carrying equipment, instruments, microphones, and amps in every direction.

Taranee took a peek at the arena. She

blinked as her eyes adjusted to the light. What a spectacle—there was so much to look at. She noticed a large screen suspended above the stage; hundreds of colorful lights; and the huge crowd. She imagined the adoring, mostly teenage fans preparing their lungs for screaming. Banners dotted the crowd. One read *A Kiss for Karmilla*. Another read *Karmilla is Queen!* Taranee could see the excitement in the air. And the concert hadn't even started yet.

Taranee was glad she had remembered to bring her camera. She had really been getting into taking pictures lately. She and Hay Lin were both in Mrs. Vargas's extra-credit photography class at school. One of their recent class assignments had been to stand outside in the blustering snow and photograph stalactites. Karmilla should be a much more interesting subject than a few dinky icicles, mused Taranee.

"Over here, girls," Mr. Lair called. While he appeared tall and bulky in his blue uniform and cap, his face looked more nice-guy than tough-guy. "Okay," he instructed, "stay put, and try not to cause any trouble."

"We can't thank you enough, Mr. Lair,"

Taranee piped up, tossing a rainbow-beaded braid over her shoulder.

"My pleasure, ladies," he replied with a toothy grin. "Enjoy the show."

But the three of them were no longer paying much attention to him.

"*Over there! Look!*" Irma screeched, shooting her arms into the air and waving them fiercely.

Taranee focused on what Irma was pointing at. "We already are," Taranee whispered, answering Mr. Lair. A big smile spread across her face.

"Danny! Danny! Daaaaaanny!" everyone howled in unison, waving their arms as Karmilla's one and only bassist walked by.

Taranee couldn't believe how cool he looked. She noticed his red bandanna, tied snugly around his long, thick, brown hair; his wide, grungy sideburns; his cute, upturned nose; and his decisively worldly aura. He was holding a bag of potato chips, and he munched continuously as he skipped down the stairs into a private, underground room. He didn't react to the earsplitting screams, but Taranee knew he must have loved the attention.

There's nothing like a fan's being in the same building with her favorite artist, thought Taranee, doing an excited little dance.

Mr. Lair turned to his daughter and her friends in complete shock.

"Wh—what is wrong with all of you?" he asked, bewildered.

"Did you see him?" Irma squealed. "It was Danny Doll! The bass player of Karmilla! And if he's here—"

"Karmilla has to be close by!" Cornelia cried, finishing the thought.

As Irma's father stood there speechless, a policeman raced over.

"Is everything all right, Sergeant?" the young, freckle-faced officer asked Mr. Lair. "Do you want me to arrest these delinquents?"

"No need for that, Spud!" Mr. Lair said with a chuckle. "This is my daughter, and these are her best friends."

And with an embarrassed shrug, Mr. Lair looked back toward them.

"Okay . . ." Mr. Lair said to the girls, attempting to stay calm. "Try not to make me look bad. You're here to *see* the show, not *stage* one."

"We promise!" they all said solemnly and in unison, putting on their most angelic smiles.

But, not even a second later, it started all over again.

"Look!" they all cried together. "There's Matt!" The three of them immediately bunched together, craning their necks past Irma's father to get a better look.

The two policemen glanced at each other. Spud looked particularly surprised—and a little frightened—by the girls' reaction.

"Forget what I just said," Mr. Lair grumbled to Spud, throwing up his hands. "If you want to throw them in jail, go for it. I wouldn't blame you."

Meanwhile, Taranee and her friends were unable to take their eyes off Matt and his Cobalt Blue band members as they strutted by in the company of a few security guards. Matt talked with a woman from Futuredome's staff. She was holding a binder in one hand and a pen in the other.

"He must be so nervous," Irma guessed, grabbing Cornelia and Taranee's hands in delight. "He didn't even see us!"

They were giddy. They couldn't help jumping up and down a few times—which wasn't easy for Cornelia, who was sporting an ankle-length green skirt.

"To open for Karmilla is a huge responsibility," Taranee acknowledged. Karmilla was an international sensation. Cobalt Blue, while incredibly edgy, hip, and talented, was just a local high school band.

Taranee felt bad that Will couldn't be there, too. She fell silent for a moment. Will would have loved that moment more than any of them. Even though Will tried to keep it a secret, they all knew she had a serious crush on Matt.

Taranee was able to relate to that. She hadn't exactly shared the secret of her crush on Nigel with her friends yet, either.

"Give me the camera!" Irma said, yanking the camera that hung from Taranee's neck, which in turn pulled the neck strap—and Taranee—right along with it. "I want to take a picture of Matt for Will."

"Ooof!" Taranee cried, starting to choke. Pushy Irma strikes again, she thought, shaking her head.

Irma held the camera up to her face, aimed

it at Matt, and snapped the shutter. Off went the flash—*click!*

"Aha!" Irma sang out. "I can already imagine Will's face when she sees this."

Taranee looked back at Irma and rolled her eyes. Irma was always ready with a funny quip, she thought. And even though two of my best friends aren't here, I have a feeling this night is going to be unforgettable.

SIX

Will slumped down in her chair. She was sitting at the kitchen table with her mom, where they had just finished dinner. The table was set beautifully—with a blue linen tablecloth and elegant dishes—but the meal was tense. Not a very festive birthday party, thought Will.

Will was trying to be nice. It was her mom's special day, after all. But she couldn't help the way she was feeling—trapped at home, left out from the best concert of the year, and angry with her mom.

Will had to admit that she was frustrated with herself, too. She didn't particularly like the way she was behaving—she wished she could cheer up and make the night fun for her mom. But it just wasn't happening.

Her mom had cleared the dinner plates and was now carrying a strawberry-chocolate cake to the table.

"What?" Will asked, trying to sound cheerful. "No candles?" Will rested her chin in her hands. It was hard to fake happiness while bumming out.

"No candles," her mom answered briskly, cutting a slice for Will. Her hair was pulled back, and she wore big, gold, hoop earrings and a lavender sweater set. She looked pretty, thought Will. And she'd have looked even prettier if it hadn't been for the seriously worried expression on her face.

Will wasn't hungry. She stuck out her hand and pushed the plate of cake back toward her mother.

Her mom picked up the plate and looked at Will coolly. "If you don't want it now, you can have it later," she said.

"I won't want it later, either," Will grumbled, standing up. She squeezed her napkin in frustration and tossed it onto the table. "I'm not hungry, Mom!"

Her mom looked surprised at the way Will was acting. But Will couldn't help it.

"Will . . ." said Mrs. Vandam, with a determined glare.

Will felt that glare burning through her.

I need some fresh air, she thought.

"Come on, dormouse," Will said, "let's go for a walk." She slipped on her winter jacket. Like a puppy, the dormouse jumped up and followed behind her.

Will's mom sat at the table clutching her napkin anxiously.

She thought her mom was probably thinking of something to say to stop her, so that Will wouldn't leave angry. But Will wouldn't turn around. She was too frustrated. Instead, she walked out with her pet and let the door shut behind her. *Slam!*

Gently placing the dormouse in her backpack, she hopped onto her red mountain bike. As she pedaled along, she wondered what her friends were doing at that exact moment. Were they dancing and singing to Cobalt Blue? she wondered.

Will steered her bike into the park. A cool, crisp breeze ruffled her thick, red hair. Will wished she'd brought her winter hat.

She stopped, leaned her bike alongside a

park bench, and sat down on the cold metal. She placed her dormouse, which was still snuggled in her backpack, down next to her. It watched her closely with its big, brown eyes.

Will shoved her hands deep into her coat pockets.

Boy, it's really cold, she thought with a shiver.

She noticed how the snow blanketed the flower beds while covering only parts of the bare trees. She spotted a man in a big-hooded parka, with ski gloves on, walking his dog nearby. Seagulls flew overhead in the distance, their cries spreading across the big gray sky.

"It's a sad Sunday," she said aloud, chewing on her zipper, "when I look forward to Monday."

She turned toward her dormouse. "That's probably the first time that has happened to me since we moved to Heatherfield," she said. She gave her pet a little smile. The dormouse looked back at her, as if it completely understood everything she was saying.

I hope Hay Lin is enjoying herself, she thought, remembering her homebound friend. At least *she* decided not to go to the concert—

while somebody else made my decision for me!

Will took out her cell phone and punched in Hay Lin's number. *Beeep-bip-beep-beep-bip.* She listened as the line rang. *Briiiinnng-briiinnng.*

Hay Lin's dad answered the phone. He sounded frazzled. She could hear the bustling sounds of the Silver Dragon in the background—it sounded like a really busy night for the restaurant. She listened as he called out, "Hay Lin! Phone call for you!"

She heard Hay Lin holler back to her father in her chipper way: "I'll take it upstairs." And then Will thought she heard her say, apparently to some customers, "Do you think you can handle this all by yourself? It's easy, just write the order, and give it to the cook. I'll be right back!"

Ha! Will giggled at her friend's gutsy resourcefulness. She could just picture Hay Lin with her sleeves rolled up, wearing a Silver Dragon apron, and handing the order pad and pen to a customer. That Hay Lin! Will could only imagine what Hay Lin's serious father would think of that stunt.

A minute later, she heard Hay Lin pick up

the phone—it was much quieter now. Hay Lin must have been in her bedroom, Will guessed.

"Will!" Hay Lin cried out excitedly. "How are you? Did you and your mom make up? Huh?"

"No," Will said, feeling embarrassed about the whole thing. She petted the dormouse.

"What are you talking about?" Hay Lin asked, sounding worried.

"I'm talking about the fact that we are still fighting!" Will answered, a bit more sharply than she had intended. "It's difficult to explain. Nothing is wrong, specifically," Will continued, biting her lip. "I just don't want to make up with her quite yet. . . ."

Hay Lin started getting worked up. She told Will that she had to apologize to her mom and make up with her.

"Please, Hay Lin!" Will begged. "Don't yell at me, too." Okay, maybe Hay Lin wasn't yelling, exactly, but Will was feeling very sensitive at the moment. "You're my friend!" Will said. "You should be cheering me up!"

"Okay, okay," Hay Lin said, returning to her usual softer, more cheerful tone. "I'll tell you something funny!"

Will could picture her friend's big, excited grin—the one she always got as she geared up to tell a story.

"Listen . . ." Hay Lin said.

All of a sudden Hay Lin stopped talking. Then Will heard "Uh-oh . . ."

"Will!" Hay Lin blurted out. "The map of the twelve portals is flashing!"

"That's not really funny, Hay Lin," Will said, rolling her eyes. This wasn't a time for pranks.

"It isn't supposed to be funny!" Hay Lin screamed, sounding surprised and serious. "It's an emergency!"

Will thought of the map, which Hay Lin always kept in her red backpack. When a portal opened up, the map flashed an enigmatic, orange light right in the spot where the dangerous action was happening in Heatherfield.

"A portal has opened up somewhere inside the stadium!" Hay Lin yelled, after studying the map for a minute.

The two friends each quickly got off the phone. Will sprang into action, picking up her backpack, with her dormouse still tucked inside, and ran to her bike.

"So, I guess I'm going to the stadium after

all," she whispered to her dormouse. "Mom is not going to be happy if she finds out. I'll have to get home early, before she becomes suspicious."

Will hopped on her bike and pedaled over to the Futuredome stadium. As she got closer, she realized how huge the building was. Breathlessly, Will navigated through the parking lot, stopping and locking up her bike on a rack that stood next to some large parked trucks.

She cradled her dormouse in her arms, threw on her backpack, and headed toward the stadium entrance. "Hopefully, Hay Lin will be able to come and help me soon, since I have no clue where the other girls are," she murmured into her dormouse's ear. "I guess, for now, I've got to do this by myself."

Will spotted the security guards surrounding the doors—two big guys with badges, buzz cuts, leather jackets, and old T-shirts that stretched across their broad chests. One had his arms crossed and wore a tough expression. The other was hollering into his walkie-talkie. Definitely not brain surgeons, Will concluded.

First I have to figure out a way inside, she

thought, hiding behind some trucks. Without a ticket, she doubted those two goons would let her just waltz in.

But then an idea popped into her head. Maybe the Heart of Candracar could help. She carefully held her palm out and concentrated. Soon, the pink orb appeared, shining its beautiful light. "Close your eyes, dormouse," she whispered. But she could tell the dormouse was surprised at what it saw.

Then, *fwooosh!* Will felt a surge of heat in her hand. Within seconds, the warmth morphed into jets of electric energy shooting up her arms and down her legs. The familiar pink energy swirled around her body, making her grow taller and stronger. She felt her flower-petal wings emerge from her back as an electric thrill tingled down her spine. Her slender body pulsated with strength and with rings of cosmic energy. The swirls softly disappeared, and a new Will emerged, having been transformed into her magical, Guardian self. She was filled with an awesome sense of power.

She peered over at the guards to see if they had noticed, but they seemed totally unfazed.

Her dormouse, on the other hand, looked

pretty shaken up. It was hunched over, with the hair on its back sticking straight up. "*Eerck!*" it muttered, a worried expression on its face.

"Don't make that face, dormouse," she whispered to the creature sweetly. "This is something I have to do."

Her dormouse looked back at her curiosity. It seemed less afraid.

Will put her hand to her head, brushed the hair away from her forehead with her fingers, and closed her eyes.

"Now, Heart of Candracar," she called out. "*Make us invisible.*"

Www-zap!

Will quickly glanced down at her hands, her body, and her feet, mightily satisfied at the results of her magic powers. It was as if a clear force field surrounded her body, making her completely invisible. Yes! she thought gleefully. It had actually worked! This was the best she had felt all day—brave and strong. The evening was turning out to be pretty fun after all.

Her dormouse looked a bit perplexed, though, and stuck its snout out of the force field, making itself suddenly visible. Will wondered what that must have looked like to anyone watching—the head of a dormouse, with no body, just suspended in air. The dormouse started sniffing the air inquisitively, wiggling its whiskers. *Sniff, sniff, sniff.*

"It's probably a better idea to stay inside, dormouse," Will whispered, pulling the animal back toward her. "I'm pretty sure it would scare someone to see just your nose appear in thin air!"

Once its nose became invisible again, Will clutched the animal close to her body. Then she took a breath and flitted right past the bouncers and into the stadium lobby.

The guards seemed to have no idea that Will and her pet were passing by. This is amazing, Will thought, smiling.

So, where do I start? Will wondered, gazing around at the enormous—and packed—building. There was no way a portal could have opened up unnoticed. That meant that the new opening must have been hidden.

She wandered around the stadium and soon found a door that led to a staircase.

The basement of the stadium, she thought.

As she descended the dark, dank, cement staircase, she passed a bunch of pipes and a sign that read *Danger*. She held the dormouse a little closer to her. At the stairway landing, she peered down at the crates and boxes piled up just about everywhere.

Well, it looks more like a warehouse than a basement, she mused. Might be just the right place. Plus, my odd sixth sense is telling me to go down there, so . . .

Suddenly Will felt a sharp ache in her temple—a swirling sensation, a concentrated dizziness.

Uh-oh . . . it's that weird feeling again, Will thought. The one that I feel whenever I am near a portal. I must be close, she guessed, poking her head through a metal door that was slightly ajar. Very close.

SEVEN

Raven towered over the Meridian rebels. He was practically double their size and rather menacing in his long, red, hooded cloak. He turned and grinned at the green monster men, women, and children who followed innocently behind him.

My plan is working well, he mused.

Together they approached the portal—the one leading to the warehouse in the Futuredome stadium. They were in Meridian now, Raven thought gleefully, but soon they would be in Heatherfield.

He led them along a brightly lit tunnel with a low ceiling. The sides were padded with a foggy, blue mist, and several puddles covered the ground.

Raven suddenly noticed sparks flashing and swirling just ahead of the group. "A portal, at last," he sighed delightedly. He spotted several boxes and crates crammed on the other side. The warehouse.

"Come on!" Raven called to the group in an authoritative voice. "Freedom is near!" He was making his best attempt to be friendly. It wasn't easy for him.

Raven extended his hand in the direction of the Meridian people. But they hung back, huddling behind his flowing, red cloak in fear. They stared wide-eyed at the now flaming opening.

He had to admit, he would not be so eager to travel to the other side, either, through a passageway like that.

"What?" Raven smiled slyly, flashing his sharp teeth. "Don't you trust me?"

He glared at the mass of Metamoorians with their green, scaly bodies; pointy, webbed ears; innocent grins; and old, ragged clothes. They looked extra disheveled after their long walk.

"It's not about trust, Raven," a Meridian rebel answered, looking perplexed. "Your offer is tempting. But crossing the portal now could be a big mistake!"

"What are you saying?" Raven ranted, poking his wrinkled, green face out from his hood. "Do you want to stay in Meridian? Do you want to be miserable and hungry? If that's the case, then I will leave you alone."

"No, no," another creature said shyly, rubbing his green facial spikes. "That is not it. . . . But Caleb . . ."

"Caleb! Caleb!" Raven burst out dramatically, his yellow eyes practically popping out of his head. "Caleb is all talk and no action, while I offer you a way of escape." He was starting to get impatient with them.

"Caleb is one of us!" another Meridian creature piped up.

"But I'm more powerful than he is!" Raven smiled smugly. "I can open an old passageway in the Veil with my magic. I've already done it in other parts of Metamoor." He softened his tone. "And now I've arrived in your city, to help you," he continued. "Join me. Leave Phobos and his cruel ways behind you!"

The creatures of Meridian now stood just before the threshold. They looked at each other with uncertainty. They seemed tempted, but very afraid.

"Nobody will notice us," Raven said, trying to lure them along. "Right now, as we speak, a large number of earth people have gathered together," he continued encouragingly. "If we disguise ourselves well enough, we can blend in with them—we can escape."

Just then, Raven sensed a stranger nearby. He gazed around wildly but saw no one. Who could it be? he wondered.

"Silence!" Raven shouted to the rebels. As soon as he waved his hand, the rebels fell silent. "There is someone here." He needed to concentrate. He needed to focus his magic powers if he were to pick up on any impending danger.

It's amazing what I can do with one simple gesture, Raven mused proudly. My power is growing. And my plans will soon be realized!

EIGHT

Oh, no, thought Will. The people of Meridian are rebelling!

Will sat crouched behind a stack of boxes and crates. She was invisible, but she hid herself anyway. She hugged her dormouse in her arms and cuddled him close to her.

She peeked out inquisitively at the tall, authoritative, red-cloaked creature named Raven. He seemed to sense Will's presence. But who was he, she wondered? She had never seen him before.

Whoever he was, she thought, he was up to no good. Leading the Meridian people through the portal could have been catastrophic for them.

"I have to find the other girls," she

whispered anxiously to her pet. "There is no time to lose!"

Will stood up, preparing to go and find her friends upstairs at the concert. But as she turned to leave, she accidentally crashed into a cardboard box, making a loud *thump!*

Oh, no! Will thought, terrified. What should I do?

"Whoever that is," Raven snarled, upon hearing the sound, "they have hidden themselves well." He walked around the warehouse, peering around boxes and inside crates. The Meridian creatures stood back and watched. "But I can still feel them," Raven added.

Now the red-cloaked creature was walking right toward Will. And he was looking right at her—well, through her, actually. She was still invisible. Phew, she breathed gratefully.

She couldn't help staring back at Raven. He was definitely ugly—a big, green, wrinkly face, sharp teeth, and scary, red-rimmed eyes. She squirmed at the sight of his long, green fingers and sharp nails as he grabbed a nearby box.

Will was nervous. And her little pet was, too. She could feel its heart thumping quickly against her chest. The dormouse must have been *really* freaked out, though, because, the next thing Will knew, it had jumped right out of her arms. In doing so, the dormouse passed right through the invisible force field, becoming wholly visible. Dormouse! she thought, horrified.

"Flashes of Imdhal!" Raven hissed, stepping backward with surprise as the dormouse flew by him as if appearing out of thin air. "Where did this come from?" he asked, befuddled.

"*Gnik!*" the dormouse squealed, running past Raven and weaving among the crowd of Metamoorians.

"Stop that creature!" Raven ordered the group angrily.

"Aaagh!" a rebel cried, shaking in fear.

"Yikes!" yelled another, lifting his foot and jumping out of the way.

Will watched a few rebels scrunch up their shoulders in panic, as others held their hands in front of their faces.

Raven turned toward the rebels. "Cowards!" he growled angrily. "Are you really afraid of this creature?"

"B—but it's so . . . *hairy!*" one of the rebels

confessed. "Have you ever seen anything so *horrible?*"

Will had to laugh. To think that these big, burly, green monsters were frightened by her sweet little dormouse—it was pretty ridiculous.

But then, she noticed the dormouse taking off toward Meridian.

Oh, no, Will thought with dismay. My dormouse has gone through the portal. Come back, Will pleaded silently from the bottom of her heart. Please, come back quickly!

But it was no use. She watched with dread as the agile little critter ran full speed through the streets of Meridian. It leaped over a pipe and into a narrow street covered by stone arches, hopping cheerfully over a few mud puddles.

Wow! thought Will, chasing after the dormouse at breakneck speed. Who knew it could run so fast?

She followed the creature up a flight of stone steps and past a pack of Metamoorians. She ran faster, afraid she'd lose it among the dark, twisting streets and decaying houses.

Maybe if I call it, the dormouse will stop,

she thought. But how would I do that? she wondered, sprinting past a high, stone wall. I've had it for a long time, and I still haven't given it a name! When—and if—I get home, the first thing I'm going to do is name the little thing.

She followed her pet as it trotted between two Meridian creatures. Having lost all patience at this point, Will cried out, "That is enough! Stop!"

Two passersby looked shocked to hear the disembodied voice.

"Are you speaking to me?" a long-haired, prickly monster demanded threateningly of a scaly, green creature. "If you wanted to be funny, you picked the wrong person to play with!"

Oops, Will thought, wincing, as she glanced over her shoulder. She hadn't meant to start a fight! Covering her mouth with her hand, she reminded herself to keep quiet.

She ran a bit further and finally, standing on top of a little hill, spotted the dormouse. It stood up innocently on its hind legs, wagging its tail.

You little beast, she thought as she rushed

over to the dormouse. I guess getting into trouble is your specialty. . . .

Will was perspiring from having chased the critter through the caves. She wiped the beads of sweat from her forehead as she tried to catch her breath.

"Are you finished with your game yet?" she asked, stepping closer to her pet. She noticed that it was looking up at a dragonfly that circled and buzzed around its head.

"Gotcha!" she cried, bending down and tackling the dormouse from behind. She grasped its body in her hands. "You've done enough damage for today. Do you realize how much trouble you've gotten us into?" she asked, picking the creature up by the scruff of the neck like a cat. "Never do that again, understand? Never!" She held the little animal up to her chest. The dormouse was now back in the field of invisibility with her. Phew! She exhaled. Safe again!

"We could have been discovered by the soldiers of Meridian!" She scolded, shaking her finger. The dormouse looked around slyly. "We could have been arrested or . . . or . . ." Will paused. She was suddenly distracted.

Black rose petals were tumbling gently

down around her. ". . . Oh, my goodness," she cried, marveling.

She looked up and saw that she was in a forest of beautiful flowers. A soothing, blue light glowed nearby. Will had never seen anything like it. She moved closer to the flowers.

"Wow," she whispered, looking closer. "Black roses!" Tangled hedges of black buds and opened flowers grew everywhere she looked, and their petals shimmered with a gorgeous, rich, deep, pitch black color. Like velvet, she thought.

But there was something slightly menacing about the plants, with their long, sharp thorns. Will leaned back to see where the seemingly endless cluster of hedges stopped. "There are . . . thousands!" she cried in disbelief.

She bent over to smell one of the flowers. "But I don't think these are your average roses," she said to the dormouse. "I sense something strange about them. This place must be protected by a kind of spell. . . ." The dormouse stuck its little nose inside the rose, too. She could hear it take a whiff.

All of a sudden, Will felt a small, sharp pain in her finger. *Swip!* It was as if a thorny branch had reached out and wrapped itself around her arm and hand.

"Ah!" Will gasped, releasing the dormouse from her hands. It jumped safely to the ground "I—it pricked me!" Will cried. She clenched her fingers against the pain. "I—I . . ." Will felt dizzy. "What's happening to me?" she breathed. Her dormouse was worried, too. It propped its front legs against her boots and looked up at her.

Will quickly grew very sleepy. She fell backward on the ground between some vines—bump!—and fainted. The magic shield disappeared, and Will was once again visible.

As Will fell, she closed her eyes. She clasped her hands beneath her cheeks to make a sort of pillow and curled up on her side. Her red hair fell loosely around her face. Half unconscious, she felt her dormouse crawl over to her. "Hmm! Hmm," it sniffed. Black petals continued to scatter around the two of them as they rested.

The dormouse nudged Will's cheek. She began to come to, and struggled to open her eyes. She saw the little critter's black eyes, grown wide with fright.

Will saw a long, black shadow loom over the two of them. She brought her hand toward her face to cover her eyes.

But Will could not fight her fatigue. Before she knew it, she was fast asleep.

NINE

"Do you think you could finish drying the plates, Dad?" Hay Lin asked. She, her dad, and Fang were cleaning up the kitchen of the Silver Dragon. The soapy sink was now almost empty of plates, cups, and chopsticks. Hay Lin wiped her brow—it was pretty steamy in there.

They were all exhausted.

"Certainly, Treasure," her dad answered sweetly, looking over his glasses. He held a wet dish in one hand and a towel in the other. She could tell her dad was surprised by her request. Hay Lin usually always completed the job at hand. "But . . ." he began.

Before he could finish, Hay Lin tossed her towel down on the counter. "Thanks, Dad," she sang out over her shoulder, pushing open the kitchen doors with the little round windows.

Hay Lin bounded up the stairs two at a time, untying her apron as she went. She wondered if Will had managed to get into the stadium without any trouble.

She ran to her room, picked up her orange phone, and dialed Will's number. I really hope she's okay, she thought.

Hay Lin listened as the phone rang. *Briing-briiing.* "Come on, Will," Hay Lin whispered. "Pick up!"

Hay Lin felt tense and worried. She bit her lip and looked out her bedroom window as she waited for Will to answer.

She noticed that the Heatherfield sky was gloomy and gray. Dramatic clouds rushed overhead as a powerful wind sailed past some bare branches. Hay Lin's eyes focused on a breezy gust below as it pulled a few dry leaves and some paper up toward her window.

The streets were empty except for one passerby who clutched his coat close as he crossed the street into the wind.

Finally, Will's phone stopped ringing. A shiver of hope and excitement ran through Hay

Lin's body. *The person you wish to speak to is unavailable at this time*, the voice on the recording stated. *Please try again later*.

"Unavailable!" Hay Lin cried out in disappointment. She hung up the phone and tossed the handset on top of a pile of sparkly Magic Markers on her desk.

Now she was worried. Why was Will not answering her cell phone? she wondered. She paced nervously back and forth in her room. Then she plopped down on her bed. Her shoulders hung heavy with despair as she sighed and stared down at the floor.

"Where are you, Will?" she wondered aloud.

TEN

"*Will!*" Voices were calling to her from both near and far away.

Who—or what—were they? Will wondered, groggily. She was floating in a dreamy, blue cloud.

And wherever she looked, all she saw were those strange, black, rose petals.

"*Will!*" chanted the voices, now surrounding her. "*Will*," they begged.

What did they want? They sounded so desperate.

A thorny branch wrapped itself around her shoulder and across her winged back. "Ow!" she cried.

"*Will!*" Again, she heard her name, this time echoing even louder around her.

Then a long bramble formed cuffs around her wrists and ankles. Another bound itself around her tummy and legs and made several loops around her tall boots. Will trembled. It was as if the branches had formed a web around her, suspending her in midair.

I'm a prisoner to a never-ending tangle of roses, she thought with horror.

"*Will, take us with you!*" howled the voices.

Aha, Will contemplated, I know who those voices belong to. It's those velvety, black roses.

They're so humanlike, she thought. The branches are like arms, and the buds are like faces.

She wriggled hard, trying to break free.

"*Will! Will! Don't abandon us!*" the voices begged in unison.

"Leave me alone!" Will shouted, terrified. "I want to get away!"

And then, with a burst of energy, she managed to free one wrist from the grasp of the brambles. But the rest of her remained entangled.

Will concentrated and flexed her muscles, attempting to wrest her body from the tight grip of the plant. "I want you to leave me alone!"

she shouted bravely, summoning up a burst of power.

The rosebush suddenly let her go.

But there was nothing to support her.

"N—No!" cried Will, free-falling into emptiness. "Noooooooooooooo!" she wailed, plunging down, down, down through the long, dark space. Her arms and hair flew up with the force of the fall, and her legs flailed behind her. She tried to use her wings, but they were helpless against the fierce speed of her fall.

Then everything went black.

Moments later (or was it hours? she wondered), Will slowly lifted an eyelid with a dazed flutter. Then she carefully opened the other eye. She was nearly blinded by a bright light that cut across the darkness and spilled over her. She quickly shut both eyes.

She felt hot and sweaty and really out of it. Had it been a dream? she wondered, still enraptured by what had just happened.

The grass felt soft beneath her. She stretched out her arms and wiggled her toes. Then she blinked and opened her eyes again, a little wider.

That light is so bright, she thought.

Gazing around, she caught sight of a few flowers that were growing nearby.

It must have been a dream . . . she concluded, lifting her hand to her brow.

A bit more alert now, she looked around again. "B—but . . ." she gasped. There weren't just a few flowers, she realized. She was inside a garden—a beautiful, enormous, extraordinary garden.

She rubbed her eyes rapidly.

The colors were exhilarating: lush pinks, rich yellows, vibrant oranges, and the most deluxe purples and blues imaginable.

It was a fantastic mix of the healthiest, most luxurious plants she had ever seen. But these were plants she had never come across before. There were hyped-up hydrangeas; unique varieties of anemones, peonies, and begonias; and snapdragons and sunflowers that seemed to burst beside her. Her heart skipped as she spotted rows and rows of too-good-to-be-true daisies and lilies. And the smell—it was intoxicating!

"Where am I?" she whispered, a bit apprehensive. She sat up and rubbed her eyes again, gazing around wide-eyed. Not too far off in the distance she spotted a beautiful castle. Its Gothic spires, arched windows, and elegant staircases appeared to shimmer, adorned with crystals and diamonds.

How did I get here? she wondered.

Suddenly, she heard a squeak. A familiar squeak. It was her dormouse, running right toward her.

"Oh, dormouse," she squealed with delight. "So, you didn't leave me, after all!"

As it got within reach, Will picked the dormouse up in her arms and squeezed it tightly to her chest. She could hear it purring. She patted its head gently. Boy, was she happy to see the little guy!

For a moment, Will wondered if she should have stayed safe at home with her mom. This place was definitely weird—and who knew what would happen next?

Be brave, be brave, she told herself.

Oh, no—now *what* was that? Will wondered, as she heard heavy footsteps behind her. They sounded like the footsteps of a giant. "Uh-oh . . ." Will said, panicking, as she looked up suspiciously.

In front of her stood a tall man with long,

gray hair pulled back in a ponytail. He had a large, green face with a brown goatee, and he had gentle, brown eyes with red circles around them. He wore brown leather boots, gardening gloves, and a purple shirt that billowed from beneath a blue vest. In one hand he held a hoe, and in the other, plant clippings.

"Please, don't be afraid of me," he said kindly, removing a glove. "My name is Daltar. I promise I won't harm you."

Will took a closer look at the powerful but sweet-looking man. There was something fatherly about him. Even with his pointy ears and green skin, he was not at all creepy, like many of the otherworldly creatures of Meridian whom she had met in the last several months. Will felt she could trust this man.

"You . . ." he began in amazement. "You. . . survived the black roses! This is a miracle." He casually placed the hoe down. "The thorns that pricked you would have been lethal to anybody else," he continued. "But not you!"

He looked at Will. "How are you capable of avoiding their power?"

"I wish I had an answer for you," she

said, rather amazed herself. She sat up. Her dormouse rested comfortably on her lap.

"Maybe it's this . . ." Will whispered, holding her palms out steadily. "Maybe the *Heart of Candracar* protected me." The magic pink orb appeared upon one palm, emanating its beautiful, pink radiance and lighting up Will's face.

Daltar moved closer to Will to take a look. An amazed, excited expression crossed his face.

"*That* is the Heart of Candracar?" he asked, taken aback. "So does that mean that you are one of the Guardians of the Veil?"

"Yes, I am!" Will replied proudly. It felt good to admit it. "But, first—where are we?" she asked, glancing around. "What is this place?"

"This is Phobos's garden," Daltar explained, taking a deep breath.

Will noticed a barrier of black roses behind him. The sight of them made her cringe.

"Have you come to challenge the prince or to help him?" Daltar asked her with concern. "Please tell me. . . ."

Will was astonished. "Don't worry, Daltar," she said gently. "I'm not here to help Phobos." What a horrible thought, she said to herself. "It sounds like you do not admire him," she added, again addressing Daltar.

"Admire him?" Daltar spat with disdain. "I *despise* that creature more than anyone in the world!" He balled up his fist and hung his head, his face scrunched up in rage.

What a relief, Will thought. She nodded in agreement.

"There is a reason for my feelings," Daltar continued, more gently now.

Will's eyes grew wide. She felt herself grow eager with interest.

"But it's a long story," he said softly.

Will was anxious to know Daltar's srory. "I'm listening," she said.

ELEVEN

Elyon gazed into the large, oval mirror in her bedroom. Just like everything else in Phobos's palace, the mirror screamed of royal opulence, with its golden trim and platinum curlicues. It shared the same character as the rest of her bedroom, she thought, observing the arched, mosaic ceilings, the luxurious, silk drapery, and her own large, fluffy, canopy bed.

She inched closer to the mirror and studied her face. Her pale, blue eyes peered right back at her, filled with sadness and concern. Her lips formed a permanent pout. She was surprised to see that her skin was soft and clear. She had figured that, with all of her recent worrying, her face would have broken out into a sea of pimples.

She took a step back, standing tall, with her hands at her sides. Then she turned to one side to admire the ruffled white dress she wore beneath her blue cloak. She liked the way the skirt fanned out around her ankles.

Next, she straightened her shaggy blond braids, which hung loosely from a blue ribbon encircling her head. What will it be like to be the Princess of Meridian? she wondered. She ran her fingers across the emerald brooch at the neckline of her cloak, imagining all of the things she would do.

Then her eyes fell on the symbols of Phobos that adorned the front of her robe. She felt a jolt pierce her body.

She still hadn't been able to figure Phobos and Cedric out. Some of the things they said made perfect sense. And they seemed truly to care about Elyon. After all, Phobos had promised to relinquish the throne to her—and to make her princess!

But she knew other people who didn't trust the prince or his lord.

Elyon thought of Caleb and Cornelia. She remembered the time recently when she had been with them in the streets of Meridian.

"Listen to me, Princess Elyon!" Caleb had said passionately, shaking his fist in the air. "You could do a lot for this world."

Elyon had carefully studied Caleb. She understood why Cornelia found Caleb so dreamy. He was definitely good-looking, with his tousled hair and long, brown coat. His confidence and determination didn't hurt, either. As the leader of the Meridian rebels who were rising up against Prince Phobos and his regime, he exuded an attractive toughness.

Cornelia, elegant as ever, had stood behind Caleb in her Guardian outfit, complete with blue, scoop-necked top, long, flowing, purple skirt, and green, leafy wings. But her face, Elyon recalled, had been filled with worry.

Caleb had stared at Elyon with his piercing, green eyes. "Fight beside us for the freedom of Meridian!" he had said to her, fervently.

Elyon remembered feeling confused as she'd stood there staring back. She was touched by Caleb's sincerity and his concern for the people of Meridian.

The freedom of Meridian . . . Elyon repeated in her mind, meditating on that phrase for a moment.

This is all so confusing, Elyon thought. Caleb tells me one thing, Cedric another. It was as if there were two Elyons, she reflected, gazing into the mirror. Two ways of thinking, two truths.

The whole thing was eating her up inside. "Whom do I believe?" she whispered to her reflection.

She took a deep breath. Suddenly an idea came to her. Perhaps there was someone else to ask, she thought, and she blinked.

With a surge of energy, she pulled on her hood and burst out of her bedroom. She raced along the hallway, down the long, jeweled staircase, and out into the courtyard. She passed through one of the palace's piazzas, which featured an elaborate fountain. She felt a cool spray as she passed by—which caused her skirt to blow up a little.

She continued walking briskly until she arrived at the Fortress of Meridian. What a menacing sight, Elyon thought, gazing up at the tall, foreboding, green-brick structure. There were two guards standing out in front of the gated entrance, clutching daggers. They both had large, blue heads and small, beady eyes, sharp teeth, and spiky, blue mohawks.

But they were respectful, she had to admit. Both bowed to her when they recognized her.

She told them her wish.

They lifted the metal gate, allowing her to enter. One of the guards took a torch and led Elyon down into the dark dungeon. "The prisoners you wish to see are in the cell at the end of the stone path," he said, looking over his shoulder at her.

The fortress was like a dark, dingy cave. The two walked in silence, easing along a long, gloomy hall with low ceilings, past cold, stone walls, and down a winding staircase. Water dripped down on them.

Elyon gazed at her feet. She couldn't shake her sad feelings. It was as if they were rumbling deep inside of her.

Finally a prison cell appeared before them.

"I will leave now, Princess Elyon," the guard muttered in his gruff voice, bowing his head to the young girl.

Elyon stood away from the metal bars and removed her hood in the half-darkness. She felt afraid.

She let her gaze wander inside the small,

cramped cell. She saw the two prisoners, a man and a woman. They were dressed in rags; their heads were bowed. They hadn't yet realized that Elyon was standing there.

Once upon a time, these people were my mother and father, she thought, still bewildered by the idea. In some ways, they still are. I grew up with them. I loved them, in fact. But something changed. . . .

She crossed her arms and thought back to what had happened a few months before, in Heatherfield—a scene that she had played over in her mind so many times.

It was evening, and Cedric was at her house, standing with her in the family room. Elyon had a crush on Cedric. He was still in human form then—long, blond hair pulled back in a low, loose ponytail, eyes cut like sapphires, chiseled features.

He stood with perfect, even imperious, posture, as he gazed at Elyon. "They are *rebels*, Elyon," he bellowed. He leaned over, taking hold of her shoulders with his large hands, and stared into her eyes. "Two horrible creatures who took you away from your *real* home and your *real* family!" he had snarled.

Elyon stared at him in disbelief. She looked around the room. This was the room where she'd grown up—a room filled with memories of holidays, birthdays, games, and happy times. It was all very distressing.

She walked over to the fireplace and looked at several family photographs displayed on the mantel. Elyon gazed at one in particular. It was a beautiful picture of her and her parents in a pumpkin patch, smiling and laughing. She stroked the glass gently with her hand.

"This is so hard to believe, Cedric," she said, sighing heavily.

Cedric paced anxiously on the other side of the room. His long ponytail swung back and forth like a pendulum behind him.

"You will get used to your new life," he assured her in a sweeter tone than before. "I promise." Then he turned anxiously toward her. "Let's go, now," he exclaimed, bounding over to her. "Pack up your things, and get ready to leave."

Just then, the big, wooden front door of the house flew open. It was Elyon's parents. They had just come back from the store and were carrying shopping bags. Her mom's shiny, red hair contrasted against a pink coat and purple handbag. Her father looked dapper in his sweater, tie, and gray-green fall jacket.

"Elyon!" her father cried out to her. They must have been surprised to see her at home alone with a fellow older than herself, especially since, at that exact moment, Cedric had been grabbing her by the shoulder.

But they didn't know the half of it.

"What's going on?" her father demanded.

"Dad, Mom!" Elyon burst out, reaching out toward them.

"Never call them that, Elyon. . . ." Cedric snapped, stomping over to her parents.

Out of nowhere, Vathek, Cedric's big, hulking, blue sidekick, arrived on the scene. He quickly grabbed Elyon's parents around the shoulders and swept them up in his arms. They looked shocked and horrified.

". . . Because this is who they really are!" Cedric called out, holding his hand out in their direction. A burst of light shot forth from his palm, forming a giant spark of electricity around Elyon's mom and dad.

Kzzzap!

"Aaagh!" screamed her parents, shutting their eyes against the bright light.

Even Vathek closed his eyes. He, too, was irritated by the strong beam of light, but somehow he managed to hold Elyon's parents tightly.

Cedric stared back at Elyon's parents with a sly, satisfied smile. "Your little game of make-believe is over. . . ."

Elyon gasped as she looked at her mom and dad. She couldn't believe her eyes. They were still imprisoned in Vathek's arms, but they no longer looked anything like themselves. They had changed into monstrous, creepy, freakish versions of themselves.

She held her hands over her mouth in horror.

And before she knew it, Vathek carried them off—right out of their own house.

"Let's go back to Meridian!" Cedric said to Elyon excitedly, grabbing her by the hand. "Let's go home!"

That was then, she thought. And this was now.

Now, she gazed at her parents—well, her adoptive parents—again for the first time in months. Much had happened since she had last seen them, but Elyon was just as confused as ever.

Elyon's gaze wandered back over to the jail cell. Her mom and dad, still in their monstrous form, sat hunched over on a bench. Elyon took a few steps closer. They must have sensed her approach, because they immediately jumped up and ran to the front of their cell in glee.

"Elyon!" her adoptive father gasped, peering out through the rusty bars. "Is that really you?"

Elyon stared. They were obviously moved at seeing her again.

"My little girl!" he cried, gripping the bars. "How are you?"

"Come closer, honey," her adoptive mother called out endearingly, reaching her arms out toward Elyon. "Let us see you. . . ."

"Oh, Elyon," her dad crooned softly. Even though he looked like a monster, his voice was sincere and very familiar.

Elyon took a step closer. She felt lost. She looked up at their green faces, weirdly wrinkled noses, pointy, elongated ears, and coarse, snakelike hair. But what she really saw was their worry—and their warmth.

Their words . . . and their loving gestures toward me, she thought. These . . . these people still love me!

"I can't stay for long," she sputtered, falling silent for a moment. "I need you to tell me the truth. To clear things up. I need some answers. . . ."

Elyon took a deep breath. "I already know my story and the story of Meridian," she said. "Now, I want to hear the truth about Phobos—at least, your version of the truth."

Her father looked troubled. "Phobos is evil, Elyon," he said with a shudder. "That is all you need to know. He has taken over and controlled your kingdom for all these years!"

"We took you away to rescue you," her mother explained. "Not to hurt you!" Her voice sounded sweet. "Your brother is the cruel one. . . ." She gazed down despondently at the ground.

"We wanted you to grow up happy and far away from a world with no hope," she continued. "Please forgive us," she added desperately. "We did it all for you!"

The cave grew silent. It was Elyon's turn to speak.

"Phobos may have made some mistakes in the past," she said edgily. "But he's changed. He wants to give me the crown." She flashed a quick, proud smile. "If he were as bad as you say he is . . ."

"Don't trust him, Elyon," her father warned. Then he added, with a deep, intense stare, "and listen to your heart!"

Elyon scratched her head in confusion. She was relieved, touched, in fact, to see her adoptive parents. But she still had her doubts. She couldn't believe in her heart that her brother Phobos was completely evil. If he was so mean, she asked herself, then why in the world would he be planning a grand coronation ceremony for her?

"All right, prisoners!" yelled a loud, rough, booming voice behind them. "It's dinnertime! Get ready!"

Elyon noticed a guard holding up a dagger as he approached the various cells. Behind him, a few other guards wheeled a big, smoking vat of porridge.

"Lower your voice, Jarus," scolded one of the large guards, seeing Elyon. "Princess Elyon is here!"

The guard gazed over at Elyon. "Oh, forgive me, Your Highness," he said, placing his clawed hand on his burly chest and bowing as if ashamed of his behavior.

"Continue," Elyon nodded quickly, looking toward the entrance. She glanced back at her adoptive parents, who were still gazing out at her through the bars. "I was leaving, anyway."

TWELVE

Cornelia wiggled her hips in time to the power pop melodies. The hood of her orange sweat-shirt swayed back and forth along with her. Karmilla and her band were rocking the house, playing all of their hit songs—and even some catchy new ones.

What a fantastic concert, Cornelia thought, grinning giddily at Taranee and Irma.

Karmilla broke out another spicy dance tune, and Cornelia sang along, shaking her arms to the funky beat. Hey, this song might be perfect for my new skating routine, she thought. Cornelia liked to mix up her competition pieces with different styles of music. She moved her body from side to side, choreographing the ice-dance moves in her mind.

But her thoughts were interrupted by Irma and Taranee; they let out ear-piercing squeals as they executed a bouncy hip-to-hip move that nearly knocked Cornelia over. Cornelia let out a snort of laughter.

Yellow, red, and blue lights flashed in every direction. And puffs of smoke billowed from hidden machines, creating a groovy mist throughout the arena.

Cornelia looked out at the throngs of fans who expressed their devotion in tears of joy and wild dancing. Their screams, whoops, cheers, and shouts at times practically drowned out the music. Everyone was enraptured and jumped up and down together to the rhythms of Karmilla's tunes.

A mosh pit had started in the middle of the arena, with the band cheering its members on. A few plucky fans tried to get onstage, and Karmilla didn't seem to mind. In fact, she pulled a gaggle of teens up onstage with her and rocked and partied with them.

So much energy, Cornelia giggled. What a spectacle!

It looks like she's having a blast, Cornelia thought.

Cornelia looked up at the big screen above the stage. She could just see it from where she and her friends danced backstage. It showed a close-up of Karmilla, singing her heart out into the microphone. Cornelia loved the way the lead singer's tight, black, high-collared jacket billowed out at the sleeves and hips. And those zebra-striped tights looked very cool as Karmilla pranced and prowled around the stage. What a hipster, mused Cornelia, noting the singer's spiky necklace.

The other band members rocked, too. Cornelia was amazed by the shaggy-haired, blond drummer. Not only did he have amazing rhythm, but he was also a lot of fun to watch, with his wild shakes of the head and his noodlelike body. She was fascinated by Danny Doll, too, as he leaned back casually and played a riff on his electric bass guitar. He looked like a real rock star in his flared pants, bandanna, and sideburns.

A slow song came next, and Cornelia fell into a bit of a rhythmic trance as she listened to the fine-spun, summer-breezy ballad. The song's romantic rhythm contained a touch of melancholy, and the innocent, young-love lyrics made Cornelia think of Caleb.

She was thankful that she had finally gotten to meet her crush in Meridian. It had been, literally, a dream come true. Caleb had been appearing in her thoughts for months, but she had not been sure he had ever really existed. Still, her instincts—and her pitter-pattering heart—had been correct, after all.

Caleb was the real deal.

He was so brave, she thought, remembering how confidently he had led the Meridian rebels to safety.

She swooned as she remembered the perfect, white lily he had given to her as a parting gift. She had kept the sparkling, magic flower in her bedroom, and she'd gazed at it every night before she went to sleep.

Again, Cornelia was awakened from her daydream, this time by Hay Lin. Yes, Hay Lin. What was she doing here? Cornelia wondered.

"*Hay Lin,*" Irma cried, raising her eyebrows. "What happened to your flu?"

"I'll fill you in quickly," Hay Lin said, fiddling with her pigtails. She wore a purple jacket, hot-pink glasses that doubled as a headband, and a big grin. "And then we have more important things to talk about."

Hay Lin explained that she'd suddenly started feeling better, and her dad had offered to drive her to the concert.

After her dad had dropped her off, she said, she had raced around the stadium parking lot trying to find the right entrance. Hot and out of breath, she had finally found her friends.

Cornelia laughed, imagining Hay Lin running around like a crazed fan, dying to get into the arena to see Karmilla.

Then Hay Lin had had to figure out a way to get inside the stadium and past the security guards.

"A thick cloud of dust did it," Hay Lin said proudly. She described the little trick that she'd used and the way she had created a thick whirlwind of dust around the guards. Apparently, they were so busy coughing and gagging from the thick, cyclonelike cloud of dust—one of their hats even flew off—that they didn't even see Hay Lin sneak by.

Hay Lin, always sweet and thoughtful, told her friends she felt bad about the little trick and had internally apologized to the guards.

After that, she had rushed off to find Cornelia, Irma, and Taranee. It hadn't been easy, Hay Lin explained, in the superpacked stadium. Hay Lin had had to push her way past swarms of dancing and cheering fans. But eventually, she'd found her friends, near the backstage entrance.

Hay Lin's face turned serious. "But right now, we have a big problem to solve," she yelled to them over the loud music. "We've got an emergency situation."

"That's beginning to sound way too normal," Taranee joked. "What happened?"

Cornelia, Taranee, and Irma stopped dancing and gathered nervously around Hay Lin.

"Somewhere in the stadium, a portal has opened," she sighed, unzipping her jacket. "I told Will, and she came here to find it, but I haven't heard from her since."

"We haven't seen her, either," Cornelia said, biting her lip. She tightened one of three barrettes that had come loose from dancing.

She thought back to the time in the recent past when she had gone to Meridian by herself. It had been really frightening. But luckily her friends had come and helped her. Cornelia understood the importance of the situation at hand—she knew the true meaning of the Power of Five.

Cornelia secretly hoped that if they went to Meridian she might get to see Elyon. She hadn't been able to stop thinking about her. And she wouldn't be upset if they bumped into Caleb, either.

"Come on," Hay Lin cried, holding out her arms. "We have to find Will! She could be in serious danger!"

THIRTEEN

Daltar liked Will's enthusiasm. She seemed like a sweet girl and genuinely interested in his story. He lived a pretty solitary life—it was just him and the flowers—and it felt good to have a captive audience.

The audience included Will's dormouse, which rested on Will's shoulder and looked up inquisitively at Daltar.

"I am caretaker of these marvelous creatures and this extraordinary garden," Daltar began. The sun was just beginning to set behind the little group.

He strolled over to a giant, pink orchid with curling petals and red and black polka dots. He touched it lovingly with his large hand. "Made for the so-called pleasure of Prince

Phobos!" he cried, shuddering at the thought of the evil prince. But then, after sniffing the pink flower, he grinned broadly with pleasure.

"So, are the black roses part of your work as well?" Will asked, standing near a vibrant, green bush. Her little pet tucked its tail around her neck, tickling her.

"Yes . . ." Daltar replied softly. "But I'm not proud of them." He looked apologetically at Will and bowed his head. "They are beautiful, yet cruel, flowers," he explained, standing before a cluster of twisting vines and pink orchids. "Pitiless flowers that deceive and betray."

Daltar wiped his brow and continued. "But I have no choice. Phobos has a hold over me and has been able to persuade me to take this role," he said with a frown.

Will listened attentively. Her dormouse stretched its neck out from its perch on her shoulder to smell a flower, allowing Will the chance to rub its little white belly.

Daltar took out a pair of shears from his tool belt and snipped a dry leaf from a flowering branch.

"I had no choice . . ." he said, his gaze growing distant. His thoughts appeared to flash back to another time.

And he began to explain how it had all started.

"I will never forget that day in the garden," Daltar said.

It was a sunny, beautiful afternoon. Daltar was watering some pink flowers, and his wife was pushing their young daughter on a swing suspended from a nearby tree. The little girl smiled and squealed with delight. She wore a summery yellow dress and yellow sandals, and his sweet wife a flowing, white frock. Both had lovely, pink roses and ribbons in their hair.

Suddenly, a voice interrupted his work. "Good afternoon, Daltar. . . ."

Daltar turned around.

There stood Phobos. He was surrounded by a group of blue-faced soldiers holding long spears.

"Your Highness . . ." Daltar said, stunned.

"I've come down for a visit!" Phobos announced, with a sly, simpering smile. He wore a long, blue, luxurious cloak. "You should feel honored, gardener," he added.

Daltar stood aghast as he watched two heartless guards grab his wife and daughter. His daughter clung to her mother and cried. The soldiers just tightened their grip.

Daltar felt as if his heart had been ripped out of his body. But Phobos just stood by, watching impassively.

Daltar looked around, panicked, trying to understand what was happening.

"I just wanted to see if the rumors I heard from the Murmurers were true," the prince said, grinning at Daltar and rubbing his red goatee.

"What are you talking about, your Highness?" Daltar asked, trying to control his anger. "I don't know what you mean. . . ."

"I want you to create roses with lethal spines," Phobos commanded forcefully. He stared at Daltar with his steely, blue eyes. "An enormous barrier of flowers between my castle and Meridian . . ." He snickered as he gestured toward the garden.

Then the prince paused, allowing his words to sink in.

"And your answer is . . ." Phobos said impatiently, a phony-looking smile on his face.

Daltar was dumbfounded. "No, Master!" he

cried, mortified at the idea. "I can't do that!" As kindly as he could, he added, "I'm just a simple gardener. To protect your castle you need strong walls—not flowers!"

"Maybe a little encouragement will make you reconsider. . . ." Phobos said, narrowing his blue eyes to malevolent slits. He looked over at Daltar's family. "Your wife and daughter will make beautiful roses," he said drily.

Daltar noticed an evil twinkle in Phobos's eye as the prince strutted over to Daltar's wife and daughter. The two of them clung to each other in fear. Tears streamed down their sweet, green cheeks.

Daltar was terrified. "Your Highness," Daltar shouted, from the deepest part of his being. "I beg you . . ."

Phobos raised his hand, launching a magic ray toward Daltar's family. "Observe, Daltar," he cackled.

Kzzzzam!

A burst of wind encircled Daltar's wife and daughter. And in a flash, the two of them disappeared before his eyes.

Where they had once stood, two black roses now grew—a large flower and a small bud. A small, spiny bush surrounded them.

Daltar fell to his knees in front of the two roses and wept.

"This is what I want!" Phobos bellowed with a dark look on his face. He stood behind Daltar, quite satisfied with himself.

And that was how it had all started, Daltar said, shaking his head.

Daltar now turned his attention back to Will.

"The evil man destroyed my family," he sighed heavily. "He had won. So I created all those black roses and raised an unbreakable barrier."

Daltar had to turn away from the young Guardian. It was such a painful story to tell he was afraid he might start to cry. After all that time, Daltar still couldn't believe his terrible fate. He felt an incredible sadness in his heart.

A cloud of black rose petals cascaded down around him.

Will had been listening attentively. Daltar could tell she was sincerely concerned. Even her dormouse looked saddened by his story.

"Anyone who touched the poisonous spines was turned into a rose," Daltar explained. He was still amazed that Will had survived the black roses' thorns and not been turned into a flower herself.

"These flowers," he continued, gazing up at the rows and rows of velvety petals, "are actually the people of Meridian." He took a deep breath. "Thousands and thousands of desperate souls who have tried to get inside the castle to ask Phobos for mercy."

"So, these roses," Will asked innocently, "are alive?" She walked over toward a rosebush, observing the flowers closely and with astonishment.

"Yes," Daltar answered, with a defeated frown. "And it is my job to take care of them. Somewhere inside these thick bushes," he said, wiping his brow, "is my family."

Daltar's eyes surveyed the enormous garden, as he gazed out at the multitudes of roses. He bowed his head.

"But I don't know where," he whispered. "A long time has passed since Phobos turned them. . . . and too many roses have bloomed."

Unable to help himself, he started to cry.

Will patted his strong shoulder. "Come on, Daltar," she said tenderly.

Daltar was touched by Will's kindness. Her visit was a pleasant break from his usually miserable existence.

"But things are going to change," Daltar said, regaining his composure. "There is a rumor that someone is helping the people to escape from Meridian!"

Will looked back at him, her eyes growing wider.

"Oh, no," Will squealed, now looking worried, as if something important had just popped into her head. "I forgot!"

Daltar grew concerned. He didn't like seeing such a sweet girl so frantic.

"The portal at the stadium!" Will called out anxiously. She started running. "I'm sorry, Daltar," she cried over her shoulder. "I really have to go!"

"I will help make the passage easier for you," he said, holding his arms out. And with a *whooooosh!* he created a magic flash of light that parted the bushy barrier of black roses, allowing Will to pass through. She smiled and waved.

In the distance, through the arched opening, Daltar could make out the city of Meridian.

"Good luck, Will," he called after her, with a friendly wave. "I hope we meet again, soon!"

"Me, too!" she hollered back cheerfully. "I hope you find your family!"

And with that, she was gone.

FOURTEEN

Will walked toward the portal. She passed through the old streets and among the medieval-style houses of Meridian.

She was still amazed at the story Daltar had just told her; it was just about the saddest thing she had ever heard, and she was still pretty shaken up about it. How could Phobos be so cruel? she wondered.

Daltar had mentioned something about a rumor—a rumor that someone was helping people escape from Meridian. That was when Will had snapped back to reality and remembered what she had witnessed earlier. She knew who Daltar had been talking about. It was that ugly Raven guy. . . .

Daltar—such a sweet man, Will

thought—and helpful, too. She was grateful that he had been able to open the passage for her. And most thankful for having survived those creepy black roses.

Will was getting closer.

She soon approached a street full of Metamoorians—green-and-blue monsters with their belongings in suitcases. They huddled with their families.

Will tiptoed over a few puddles on the cobblestoned streets.

She spotted Raven standing tall in the middle of the crowd, draped in his long, red cloak. He was talking and gesturing enthusiastically. The crowd seemed excited. They cheered and hooted.

Behind Raven, Will saw the open portal. It flashed and sparked a strong, white light. The passageway was clear.

Will quickly created an invisible shield around herself again, making her and her dormouse invisible. This time she held the dormouse tight in her arms, to prevent it from escaping. She couldn't afford another mistake.

Hmmm, thought Will, moving through the crowd. What's going on here?

"So, what are you waiting for?" Raven asked the rebels, a note of irritation in his voice. "I can't keep this portal open much longer. Hurry!"

"We're worried, Raven," a spotted Metamoorian with webbed ears said. He stood back and looked out from under his large, green eyebrows in fright.

Just then Caleb and Vathek arrived on the scene. They climbed high up on a stone wall. Vathek crouched near Caleb, looking as though he might jump down at any moment. Caleb stood tall with his arms akimbo. "They are worried," he called out to Raven determinedly, "because they don't trust you, stranger! Who are you?" Caleb asked. "And why are you here?"

Caleb and Vathek leaped down from the wall in unison and sauntered over toward Raven and the crowd. The Metamoorians who had gathered there looked up at them with pure admiration.

"You . . ." Raven said, turning to Caleb with surprise. "You're Caleb. And you must be Vathek! I've heard talk of you," he added, in an unkind voice. "The famous rebels . . ." he sang out with ridicule.

"And, for our part," Caleb said, "we know nothing about you except your name." He looked mistrustfully at the red-cloaked creature.

A Metamoorian rebel piped up in an attempt to explain to Caleb who Raven was. "He's a great leader in some regions of Metamoor."

"He's also a thoughtless person who doesn't know what he is doing," Caleb said, raising his fist. His voice was strong and deep. "The world beyond that portal is not ready to welcome the people of Meridian."

Will squirmed as she saw Raven stand with his arms crossed.

"The Veil will collapse beneath the pressure of such a large crowd. . . ." Vathek explained, pointing a finger at the nearby portal.

"And if that happens," Caleb continued passionately, "the consequences for both worlds will be catastrophic!"

Will could see the anger rising in Caleb's eyes.

"You lie!" Raven yelled, turning his back to them. "That is nonsense! You are afraid that these people will follow me instead of you!"

Will listened intently.

"Come on, people of Meridian!" Raven hollered. He started moving toward the portal. "Follow me!"

"You are not to be trusted," Vathek screamed in his deep, throaty voice. He tried to stop the advance of the group with his hulking, blue body.

Oh, this does not look good, thought Will. Maybe I shouldn't reveal myself quite yet.

She was thankful for her invisible shield.

Suddenly, Raven turned around toward Vathek. "Stay away from me, you big beast!" he screamed. Surprising everyone, Raven shot a magic ray straight at Vathek.

Kzzz-zzzak!

"RAAAARRGH!" Vathek yelled, as his body was thrown violently backward and onto the ground.

Will clapped her hand over her mouth, covering a gasp.

Vathek quickly pulled himself up into a standing position. A cloud of smoke came out from the center of his chest; his shirt looked burnt. But he didn't seem to be in pain. Vathek looked determined—very determined. He glanced over at Raven.

"That voice . . ." Vathek said, stunned. Wiping the sweat from his brow, he pointed his finger right at Raven.

"That power . . . I . . . I know you!"

Raven stood there, uneasy, his red cloak blowing out around him.

"It's Lord Cedric!" Vathek cried.

"What?" a flabbergasted rebel yelled from the crowd. The others stepped back, also in sheer surprise, widening the circle around Raven.

"It's a trap!" Caleb shouted with conviction to the crowd.

Will and the others gaped as Raven, or, rather, Cedric, went through a sudden transformation. His face quickly changed and became more human. Now, three quarters of his face was Cedric's, while the remaining portion retained the monstrous aspect belonging to Raven. But he still sported the red cloak.

"You're quick, Vathek!" Cedric snapped, a bit uneasily. "We were a good team, once." He let out a harsh cackle.

"Get out of here," Vathek called out to the

group of exiles behind him, trying to scatter the crowd. "Go home! Quick! Quick!"

"Aaagh!" some of the creatures screamed, trying to escape. They scampered desperately around in a frenzy. "Eeeek!" squeaked others. A few, in their fear, even ran carelessly close to Cedric.

Will jumped every which way, trying to get out of their way.

"But all good must come to an end," Cedric continued, tucking some of his long, blond hair into his red hood. He extended his hand in Vathek's direction.

Vathek stood in front of a Metamoorian mother with a child, trying to shield them behind his huge girth.

Cedric sent out another strike, hitting the giant, blue monster's shoulder.

"Aaargh!" Vathek screamed, a painful expression on his face. He quickly fell to the ground. He was at the mercy of Cedric, who now stood over him, preparing to strike again.

"Vathek!" Caleb cried. He was busy trying to save other frightened people, so he couldn't do anything to rescue his friend.

"Good-bye, old friend!" Cedric said breezily,

stretching his hand out once again toward Vathek. He attempted to throw another magic ray. But instead, the strike hit a kind of round, clear, magic field that was now protecting Vathek.

Fzzzzak!

Vathek gasped, as he was lifted high up into the air.

"Huh?" Cedric screeched.

Will couldn't hold herself back any longer. She positioned herself between Vathek and Cedric and allowed her invisible shield to descend like a screen, revealing her from the knees up. Wavy, blue circles of energy pulsed out from around her.

The cellophanelike circle enveloped Vathek—and placed him gently on the ground. He stepped out unharmed.

Will stood up straight, holding her dormouse under one arm. She and it both gazed ahead confidently.

"Sorry to bother you," Will piped up, "Did I interrupt anything?"

"Will?" Vathek exclaimed in disbelief. He was bent double, but he looked relieved. "Where did you come from?"

"Now's not the time to talk," Will replied. She looked out at the creatures of Meridian, who were racing about, visibly upset and confused. "We have to get these people away from here before someone gets hurt."

"Your kindness is touching. . . ." Cedric growled. He was standing behind Will in his reptile form. He waved his long, thick, green tail angrily. "But maybe you should think about yourself first, my young Guardian!" he spat.

Before they knew what hit them, Cedric sent an evil strike at her, Caleb, and Vathek—KZZZAKZZZZ!

"Aaagh!" cried Will, writhing in pain.

"Unnnh!" Vathek screamed, covering his eyes.

Caleb held up his arm, trying to shield his eyes from the bright ray.

They all fell to the ground.

Cedric stood over their bodies, peering down at them with satisfaction. "Prince Phobos will be proud of me," he smirked through his fangs. "Not only will I defeat the rebel leaders, but I will get possession of the Heart of Candracar." He glared down at Will with blazing eyes. "Not bad for a day's work."

Will, Caleb, and Vathek rolled around on the ground, quivering in pain.

Suddenly Cedric let out an earth-shattering, earsplitting scream: "Yeowww!"

Will raised her head to look. Her dormouse had attached himself to Cedric's snaky tail—with its teeth—and was chomping down with a fierce, sharp bite. *Glip!*

Cedric turned to find the source of this incredible pain. "You!" he screamed at Will's furry, brown pet. "What do you want?"

Will quickly collected her thoughts. She wiped the sweat from her temples and crawled forward on her hands and knees.

She looked over at Caleb and Vathek. They both still looked a bit stunned. "Get yourself to safety!" Will cried. "I'll distract him and get him to follow me. . . ."

"No, Will!" Vathek cried. He looked worried. "It's too dangerous!"

Will stood up and ran over toward Cedric. She grabbed the dormouse, which was still hanging on to Cedric's tail—*snatch!*—and pulled her pet up under her arm. Interception, she thought gleefully, shaking her hips. "If you don't mind, I think this belongs to me," Will said, leaping over Cedric's tail and trying to stifle a giggle.

Cedric didn't know what had hit him. "Huh?" he cried, looking around him.

"If you want to catch me," Will taunted, smiling over her shoulder, "you're going to have to creep a lot faster than that, you monster!" Will started running away from Cedric, right toward the swirling portal.

"Do not underestimate me, Guardian," Cedric called out fiercely, chasing after her. Magic discharges of energy sizzled around him. *Rrrackkh! Crackle!*

Something was about to happen. Will could feel it. But she didn't know what. So she continued to run toward the portal, her dormouse tucked tightly under her arm. She glanced back over her shoulder and noticed that Cedric had transformed himself yet again. The snakelike part of his body was being replaced by a pair of strong, reptilian, muscular legs with translucent scales. Worse, an enormous pair of thick, muscular wings like those of a bat or pterodactyl had emerged from his shoulders.

"You should know by now that I am full of surprises," he called to Will.

He flapped his wings and grinned a toothy grin.

Oh, no, thought Will. He's not lying. I had no clue he had wings. . . .

The portal, thought Will, as she approached the brightly lit tunnel. She felt a rough wind pouring forth from it. I have to close it. . . . She clutched the dormouse tightly, jumped into the open portal, and put her hand up. *Whooosh!.* . . Before it's too late, she breathed.

Will landed safely on the other side—she was once again in the warehouse in the basement of the stadium. Will held up her hand and threw a magic ray against the portal in order to close it. *FZZZZAK!*

The portal closed with a streak of magic lightning.

"Face it, Will," hissed Cedric, suddenly appearing behind her, inside the warehouse. "I'm the biggest, the strongest . . . and the quickest!" He spread his monstrous wings for emphasis.

"Don't forget 'the ugliest,'" Will shouted back. But she was surprised to see Cedric standing before her.

"This is not the time for humor," Cedric roared.

They were now face to face.

Cedric held up his two claws and, looking right at Will, aimed a magic ray directly at her head. But Will shot one right back. The energy met in the middle. *KRRR-ZZZAK!*

"Aaaagh!" Will screamed, turning her head to the side and closing her eyes to shield herself from the hot sparks.

Cedric raised his muscular, green arms to throw another magic ray.

Zzzrahhkkkzzz! The rays came at Will as her dormouse escaped, frightened, looking for a place to hide.

"You and your friends have nothing," Cedric shouted. "Why don't you leave things up to the adults?" Cedric emitted a huge cackle.

This time Will couldn't react quite fast enough. She was forced to bow to Cedric's strength. Cedric's last rays were effective and full of power. *ZZZRAAAKKK ZZZRAAAAK!*

Cedric was now very close to Will.

Will summoned her powers trying to create a magic shelter to protect herself—but it was challenging.

"In the name of Phobos," Cedric commanded, now even closer to Will, "give me the Heart of Candracar, Guardian."

Will couldn't withstand the electric ray that was aimed right at her head.

"Ow!" she cried, turning away and shutting her eyes tight. "I . . . nnngh . . . I . . ."

Cedric towered over her. The only thing that separated them was Will's magic shield—which she was just then managing to create.

"Give it to me, now," Cedric hissed.

"Do you know what I have to say to that, Cedric?" Will replied calmly, while glaring back at him. She felt a surge of Guardian power.

Will could faintly hear the sounds of Karmilla from the floor above the warehouse. Her mind quickly flashed to the thought of her friends at the concert. She figured that Hay Lin might have told them that she had gone to check on the open portal.

Hurry up, she thought. She wasn't so sure how long her magic shelter would last.

She could almost imagine her friends starting to look for her. But it sure wouldn't be easy for them in that enormous stadium.

Will shut her eyes for an instant and wished

hard for her friends to find her. She really needed the Power of Five, because, in the face of Cedric's surprises and power, Will needed the magic and strength of all of the Guardians of the Veil.